colorblind

colorblind

siera maley

Published by Siera Maley in Atlanta, GA
www.sieramaley.com

Printed in The United States of America

ISBN 978-1508403043

Cover image by Robert Ramirez is licensed under a Creative Commons Attribution 4.0 License
Cover and book design by Ashley Clarke

First Edition, 2016

Chapter One

"Welcome to Daily Fries, sir, what can I get for you?"

I feigned a smile at the overweight man who stood on the other side of the counter. His eyes scanned the menu on the dirty wall behind my head as my hands hovered over the cash register in front of me. Even as he began to give me his order, I couldn't keep my gaze from darting to his forehead. The number 45 rested there, etched into his skin just an inch from his left temple. Or plastered, more like. It certainly *felt* too big to avoid looking at, even as much as I hated seeing it. No, it couldn't be on his neck, or chest, or somewhere hidden by clothing. It *always* had to be the forehead, where I couldn't avoid it.

I chewed at my lip, mentally running through

potential causes of death. Car wrecks were common, so that guess wasn't particularly creative. Maybe it'd be cancer. Or pneumonia?

I finally settled on heart disease.

"I'll take three burgers with an extra order of fries and a large coke, please," he said.

Yep. Heart disease.

"That'll be $19.32."

I was what some might've called an enabler. Heart disease was the leading cause of death in America, and yet here I was, working at a fast food place on the outskirts of San Francisco, with the literal ability to see peoples' age of death, *and* – in cases like this guy – helping make it happen.

From a moral standpoint, that might've seemed wrong. In fact, it almost certainly was. But I had a simple solution to this moral dilemma: to ignore it in hopes that it'd eventually go away. I tried not to think about it. I didn't allow myself to care about the people I was serving. Knowing when they'd die made it inconvenient to get invested, to say the least, and if there was one thing I'd learned, it was that sometimes you have to let people make their own decisions. I didn't know if Mr. Three Burgers would change anything about his life if he knew he'd be dead in a few years, but I did know that it wasn't my place to interfere. I'd tried that once. It hadn't worked.

Three Burgers got his food and left, and next up was a woman on her cell phone flanked by two small children – a boy and a girl, both about six years old. My heart dropped into my stomach.

"*Don't look, don't look,*" was my mental mantra as I took the order of the woman who'd die at age 81, but then she went back to her phone call and made her kids order for themselves, and I had to. The boy would live to be 72, but the girl would die at 51. I'd seen worse.

I gave the woman her total, and she distractedly handed me her driver's license instead of her credit card. She was trying to balance her phone call and her two young children and was having some trouble. Before I corrected her, I glanced down at her date of birth. May 19th, 1979. The year was 2015. She was 36. About thirty years older than her daughter. That 81 and 51 suddenly became a lot harder for me to stomach.

I swallowed hard as we swapped cards, and then she paid, took her food, and moved on. So did I. It was the alternative to wondering if that mother and daughter would die simultaneously from the same cause or just a few months apart from different causes.

"Harper. Chill," a voice murmured in my ear, and I felt a hand gently squeeze my arm. Robbie. I must've looked as tense as I felt.

Robbie was a twenty-two-year-old college dropout who worked here with me. He was the only person who knew what I could do, and that was because he could do it too. We'd spotted each other instantly when we'd met and just *known*. It'd been hard not to; we were both kind of obvious about our forehead obsessions. When I'd met Robbie, the first thing he'd done was to glance to mine even as I'd stared up at his. His arched eyebrow and my wide-eyed look in response had been all it'd taken to confirm we were both looking for the same thing.

Robbie would die at age 76. In the meantime, he made me promise not to tell him his number – in the irony of all ironies, we could see the number of every person we met, even when we didn't want to, but we couldn't see our own. Robbie also refused to tell me my number, which was probably for the best.

Neither of us could remember waking up one day with this awful ability. We'd both just always been this way. We had little else in common, but the side effects our special "quirk" had caused over the years – mild to moderate depression, extreme cynicism, and emotional detachment, to name a few – were enough to eventually bring us together. He was my only friend, and I wanted to keep it that way. Even people who'd die at 98 still had a visible expiration date – or at least to people like Robbie and me, anyway – and I wasn't really equipped to deal with having multiple friends whose ages of death were constantly staring me in the face. My father and Robbie were enough.

But even the two of them would die eventually. Everyone did. It was inevitable. It was one thing to know that like a normal person did: to have it in the back of my mind, only to creep up every once in a while. And when it did creep up in the mind of a normal person, there'd perhaps be a brief moment of existential crisis, and maybe some of the momentary panic or fear that comes with being actively self-aware of our own mortality. When would it happen? *How* would it happen? Would it hurt?

But for normal people, that moment would fade, and life would go on. It wouldn't for me. That moment *was* my life. It was one thing to know that we were all going to die, but it was another entirely to be reminded every time I looked at another person. Everyone was just a number to me, because that was all I could allow them to be. Anything more and I'd spend my life running around panicking about the impending expiration of the woman in the cereal aisle at the grocery store. And that was no way to live, really.

About three hours into my four-hour shift, Robbie and I took our fifteen together and sat outside in the alley behind Daily Fries, our backs pressed to the wall of the building as Robbie lit a cigarette.

"I got a woman, looked to be about early to mid-twenties. Age of death: 26," he told me.

"Wow," I murmured and ignored the wry smile he cracked. Robbie was trying to teach me to take this whole thing less seriously, so we'd started playing this awful game where we'd try to one-up each other every day. Whoever could get the most ill-fated customer won.

It was a little too morbid for me, but I humored

him. It was his way of trying to turn those very real people with very real ages of death into characters. The goal was to trick ourselves into caring less.

Sometimes, for just a moment, it'd work, and I'd forget. I'd feel a little bit better. "Uh... mother and daughter who are gonna die within the same year. Possibly simultaneously."

"How old?"

"51 and 81."

"Ah, that's not bad." He took a drag from the cigarette and then rubbed it into the wall to put it out. A black, circular blemish was visible on the white brick when he was finished. It was one of many; Robbie and I came out here five times a week. "They'll live a while."

"I guess so."

"Chill." He repeated his command from earlier. "People die. It's unavoidable. We're just two of the unlucky ones who've happened to have gotten stuck being able to see how much time they have left."

"Don't you ever think about whether or not they'd live their lives differently if they knew?" I asked him. It was the reason sometimes I wished I knew when it'd be my time to go. There were things I wanted to do. Places I wanted to see. It'd be nice to know when my deadline was. But the paranoia probably wasn't worth it.

"Of course," Robbie agreed. "But death is still inevitable. We can't change the number; it's never worked for either of us. You still lost your mother and I still lost my sister. So there's no use upsetting anyone. And besides... they wouldn't believe us if we told them. We'd just get locked up in some psych ward and ignored. It's happened before to others."

"That's true," I conceded, and tilted my head upward to stare at the sun above our heads. Summer was just beginning. I'd be starting my senior year of high school in the fall. My job here was temporary; something my dad had encouraged me to do to help save money for college expenses. In my more cynical moments, I sometimes wondered if I'd even live long enough to go to college. Or to finish college. Or to get a real job.

"Do you ever wonder why we all try so hard to live to age 80?" I asked Robbie abruptly. "What's the point? You go to school, then you live to work and work to live until you retire, and then you die, either painfully or not. And that's if you're lucky. It all seems so pointless sometimes."

"Hell if I know. They have an entire industry dedicated to making sure people don't feel pessimistic enough to ask the questions you're asking now."

"Psychiatry?" I asked.

"Religion," he corrected with a smirk, and I laughed and swatted at his leg. "What? It's so true! Religion basically comes down to 'Please don't all off yourselves; we promise you'll get rewarded for dying unwillingly instead as long as you aren't a murderer. Or a homosexual.'"

I laughed again, harder this time. "So I'm screwed then?"

"I knew it! I knew you'd killed," he joked and then moved to get to his feet. I checked my cell phone to see that we'd been outside for fourteen minutes now.

"Only indirectly," I told him, not entirely kidding.

"Stop that," he chastised. "It's not our responsibility to monitor strangers' lives. Look out for yourself, remember?"

"Yeah, I remember."

And I did. Whatever all-powerful being had chosen to assign the numbers on our foreheads – whether it was a God, or something evil, or just plain old fate – chose to give my mom a 41. She'd had me when she was 29, and she'd died four and a half years ago, when I was 12.

Before then, I'd spent years wondering how she'd pass away. In the end, it was a car wreck. I wasn't sure how I could've stopped it. Robbie liked to say that there was nothing I could've done, but I was sure he only believed that because he was convinced fate was the cause of the numbers. He was also a staunch Atheist, which seemed counter-intuitive given that the religious were all about things being predetermined, but I hadn't ever really asked him to explain further.

As for myself? I really had no idea why the numbers were there, or why I could see them. I'd done a lot of observing over the years, and I'd never seen a number change. But I'd also not developed too many long-term relationships, so it wasn't like I was checking up on people I used to know to see if their numbers were still the same.

Maybe they'd be different if I did. Maybe my out-of-shape Uncle Wayne could decide to go on a run every morning and it'd change his 73 to a 74 or something. Or maybe he would die of cancer at 73 and there was no stopping it. Maybe he would die of cancer at 73 and there *was* a way to stop it. Or maybe it'd be a car crash, like my mom, and if I ever convinced Uncle Wayne to never leave his house, I'd see his 73 jump instantaneously to an 86.

It was easy to see how I could drive myself crazy with this stuff. Which was why Robbie's advice was to just live life as though we weren't special. His sister had died of cancer, and although he didn't like to talk about it much, I'd gotten bits and pieces of the story over the course of the past few months. She'd been a couple of years older than him; only 21 years old when she'd died.

She'd had that 21 on her forehead for as long as he could remember, and he'd practically driven himself crazy trying to figure out how to change it. When she was diagnosed with stage 4 ovarian cancer at age 20, he'd realized there was no way he could have. Cancer was so rare for someone her age that he wouldn't have ever thought to suggest having her checked for it, and even if he somehow had, and even if he'd managed to get the exact type of cancer correct, no one would've taken him seriously.

I was in a similar situation with my mom's car crash. What could I have done? I'd spent the years leading up to her death trying my best. I'd told her to be safe every day when she'd left for work. If she'd gotten sick, I'd helped my dad nurse her back to health. I'd spent sixth and seventh grade having panic attacks in the night because I'd been so worried about her. And in the end, all I'd have had to do was convince her to stay home on one particular evening. But I'd had no way of knowing that for certain at the time, and now she was gone.

And maybe God/Satan/fate or whoever had known that I *wouldn't* know what to do, and maybe that was why she'd gotten a 41. And if that was the case, I had a hard time thinking well of that omniscient being. It was no wonder Robbie was an Atheist; the idea that something intelligent enough to design thinking, feeling, living creatures would then assign them unchangeable expiration dates was horrifying.

When my work shift ended, I said goodbye to Robbie and drove home to my dad. He was waiting with a plate of chicken tenders and fries and an only mildly reassuring 83 on his forehead. He would live for a long time, but I knew I'd wind up counting down the days after he hit about 80 years old. Assuming I was still around then, of course.

But I guess maybe there was always a small chance his 83 would find a way to turn into something higher. Maybe if enough time had passed. Maybe if he did something, *anything,* differently one day. Maybe if he did something that God or Satan or fate hadn't been counting on.

And I wished every day for that. To have some proof, or even just some *hope* that we weren't all essentially sitting around waiting to hit our predetermined expiration dates.

It'd be nice to have some evidence that we control our own destinies, I think.

Chapter Two

I met Chloe Stephens a day after chicken tender night, when I nearly hit her with my car.

I was lost in my own thoughts on my way to work, and had barely made it down the street from my house before I had to slam on the brakes.

She'd been chasing her escaped puppy across the street, and I came so close to hitting her that when we locked eyes through the windshield, I could see the light splash of freckles across her face and the color of her eyes. It was the first time I could remember looking at someone's eyes before their forehead. Hers were a bright blue. Her hair was blonde, and pulled up into a messy ponytail, with a couple of stray tendrils framing her face. She was cute.

She cradled the puppy in one arm and a leash

attached to a collar in the other. I didn't make the connection until later that the dog must've slipped his collar while she was taking him for a walk.

I think she was – quite understandably, really – stunned at first, because she didn't move from out in front of my car. I shifted the gear into park and scrambled out, and felt my cheeks heat up as I rushed to apologize to her.

"I'm sorry; I didn't see you," I explained hastily, my eyes still on her very, very blue ones. "You're okay, right?"

She blinked back at me, a little wide-eyed, and then turned red right before my eyes. "No, I'm sorry. That was my fault. I'm still getting used to having a puppy. Baxter here doesn't like to listen to me." She gestured to the dog in her arms.

"He's cute," I said, mostly because I didn't know what else to say. The puppy was some sort of golden lab mix, and he was struggling to get out of her arms, so she knelt down and placed him on the ground, then reattached his leash and collar.

"So do you live around here?" she asked me.

"Yeah, just down the street." I pointed to my house as she straightened back up.

"Cool," she said casually, and smiled at me as though I hadn't just nearly killed her. "My parents and I just moved in last week. I've always wanted to live in the city... especially in California. The weather here in San Francisco is so nice."

"Yeah, well... beware the people. I don't think they're as nice as they are in small towns," I warned her. "Everyone's always in a hurry."

"Right." One corner of her lips quirked upward into a smirk. "I hear they nearly hit you with their cars."

"Ouch." I pressed a hand to my chest, and she laughed at me. Then we shared a smile. There was something about her that made me comfortable in a way I wasn't used to feeling. I'd heard before that sometimes two people could meet and instantly click: instantly know they're going to get along. It was like that with her.

"Alright, well..." she said at last, still cradling Baxter to her chest, "Um, I guess you probably have somewhere to be, but it was nice to meet you, other than the whole near-death experience thing. I'm Chloe, by the way."

"I'm really sorry," I said again.

"It's fine! I'm fine...?" She looked at me expectantly, and I realized she wanted my name.

"Harper. Okay. Enjoy California, I guess."

"Oh, I will. Bye, Harper." She gave me a wave and moved to turn away, and I remembered her forehead at the last second. My eyes darted up, and in hindsight, maybe they shouldn't have. Maybe I should've let Chloe Stephens be the one untainted human interaction I'd had in years. The one person whose company I'd just enjoyed for a few easy, simple seconds without pondering depressing, existential-crisis-inducing things like her age and cause of death.

But I glanced to her forehead and swore I saw 16,

and then she'd turned away. Was walking away. And then my curiosity was getting the best of me, and I was suddenly doing something I told myself I'd never do. I was caring.

"Hey!" I called after her, and she paused to turn back again. I wasn't looking at her eyes anymore. The 16 on her forehead held my focus as I struggled to think of something to say. I'd only called her back to get another look at her number. "Um... if you need someone to show you around, I'm free most days in the afternoon," I finally blurted out.

She smiled at me again, almost slyly, and then nodded. "Okay. I might take you up on that, Harper."

"Okay. Cool."

I watched her go, and then, when she was back inside her home, I clambered back into my car and let out a heavy breath. I reached up and gripped the steering wheel so tightly that my knuckles turned white, and immediately berated myself. I'd spent so long keeping to myself, and the first person other than Robbie that I'd reached out to was a girl who'd be dead within the year. She *had* to be sixteen years old already. She looked my age, and I was seventeen.

Robbie was going to be disappointed in me.

* * *

"What exactly do you think you're going to accomplish?" he asked me just a few hours later.

"I don't know," I murmured. "It just came out. I

15

just word-vomited all over the place. I saw a cute girl and turned into an idiot. I didn't even notice her number at first."

"Who does that?" he countered, looking confused. We were on break again, and it was so hot out that I could see sweat dripping from the tips of his dark, shoulder-length hair. "You have the power to see when people will die, and you met someone and *didn't* immediately look to see?"

"She had nice eyes," I mumbled, and only felt dumber when he raised an eyebrow at me.

"Seriously?"

"*And* I'd almost run her over, too, so I was a little distracted, okay?"

"Her number was 16 *after* you almost hit her?"

"Yeah, clearly she wasn't meant to be killed by me," I told him, rolling my eyes. "Obviously it's something else."

"Something else that's happening soon," he reminded me. "The smart thing to do would be to not get attached."

"I've never been that smart," I said.

"Just don't be dumb," he told me. I nodded, understanding. No initiating contact. That was mostly fine with me. I didn't *want* to befriend a cute girl months from death. That sounded like a tragic Nicholas Sparks novel waiting to happen.... but only if she somehow found me attractive.

"She was probably straight, right?" I asked Robbie, half-kidding. He smacked me on the arm in response and rolled his eyes at me. I smiled back, and it helped. And then I tried my best to forget about Chloe, because if I thought about her too much, I'd wind up dwelling on the fact that she was a real person with a real life who had real parents that were going to be devastated when she *really* died.

As long as I didn't think about her, and as long as I didn't see her, I'd just hear about her death through neighborhood gossip, and maybe my dad and I would talk briefly about how unexpected and sad it was, and then we'd move on. Life would go on with or without Chloe Stephens, after all. It waited for no one. It never had.

* * *

My dad was a lanky, black-haired man with thick-rimmed Harry Potter glasses and a timid voice that all but confirmed he'd been kind of a dork growing up. On rainy days back when I was younger, I'd sometimes liked to sit on the couch with him and watch *Buffy the Vampire Slayer,* and we'd joke around about how he and Giles would've been best friends were Giles a real person.

Dad got even quieter after we lost Mom. He worked from home now, so he spent most of his time during the day in his office on the computer. But he did come out to make dinner most nights, and occasionally we'd watch an old movie together. I knew he loved me, but I also knew he didn't like being a single dad.

I didn't look much like him. I had Mom's

brunette hair, only mine was a slightly darker shade than hers, and a little less naturally wavy. I also had her dark brown eyes. Dad used to like to joke that he couldn't tell my pupils from my irises, but he'd stopped when he'd realized it was making me insecure. But everything had made me insecure back then. For a while, I'd been obsessed with being perfect. I'd thought that maybe if I was flawless, I'd live forever. Ten-year-old logic, huh?

During dinner maybe three days or so after I'd met Chloe, Dad perked up out of nowhere and told me, "Oh, right. I can't believe I forgot. A girl stopped by looking for you today while you were at work. It was just half an hour or so before you got home, actually."

"A girl?" I repeated quietly, although I obviously knew who it'd been. I hadn't talked to any girls other than Chloe lately. Or ever.

"A very cute girl." He wiggled his eyebrows at me, smirking, and I rolled my eyes at him.

"Dad, c'mon."

"She seemed very eager to see you. And she brought a dog along. I didn't know you'd made any new friends; does she work with you?"

"No, she's new to the neighborhood. I nearly ran over her and her dog the other day."

His eyebrows pulled together, and he studied me, concerned. "I thought I told you that if you were using my car you needed to be careful."

"I was! She ran out into the street! Besides, she's obviously fine now. It wasn't a big deal."

"Well, just make sure you're not texting and driving, or whatever it is you kids do now."

"What did she want specifically?" I asked, rolling my eyes again. "Like, what did she say?"

"Well, she asked if you lived here. I told her yes, but that you were working and would be home soon if she'd like to wait. She suggested I just tell you she stopped by, and I said that I would, and then she left."

I looked away from him and picked at my food with my fork. "Okay." There was a long silence, and then I asked him, "Do you think I should spend time with her?"

"Of course. You could use a new friend. Especially with it being summer. You have to do *something* with your free time other than working with that older guy – who I *still* have yet to really get to know, by the way. And that doesn't mean I don't think he seems nice, but I don't like the idea of your only friend being in his twenties. You're seventeen."

"Yeah, but..." I trailed off, and then shrugged my shoulders. It wasn't like I could just tell him what I knew about Chloe. There was no telling how quickly my life would spiral out of control if I did. It just wasn't ever going to be an option. I'd made a few comments about it when I'd been much younger, and the adults had laughed it off back then. They thought it was funny that I was convinced I had a special power. Now I was old enough to know that I'd never tell. "I don't know," I finally said. "What if we don't click or something?"

"Well, you'll never know unless you try."

"What if we do click and we become friends and then it ends badly somehow?"

Dad was quiet for a moment. I think, to some extent, he understood what I was getting at, because when he finally spoke again, he'd softened and reached over to take my hand with his. "Harper, I know that things have been rough. We've both been through a lot. Loss is... it's hard. But that's no reason to cut yourself off from the rest of the world just because you're scared to lose someone again."

"If you could do it all over again with Mom," I asked, looking up at him, "would you?"

"Of course."

"What if she'd died earlier? Like, giving birth to me or something?"

"That doesn't change my answer," he replied simply.

"What if you'd only been friends, and she'd still died ten years earlier?"

"Harper, people are not milk cartons," Dad sighed out. "You don't pick and choose the ones you think will last the longest without going sour. If it feels right, you just go with it until it doesn't feel right anymore. And sometimes when something goes wrong, it hurts. That doesn't mean it wasn't worth it in the first place."

I sat back in my chair, my eyebrows furrowed and my eyes on my lap, and let out a quiet sigh. Dad cleared his throat and stood, moving to clean off the dishes on the table.

"Spend some time with a girl your age who wants to get to know you. Even if it's just friendship, and even if it's just for summer. You could use the company, and I think it'll be a reassuring experience for you when nothing bad happens and you make a great friend. She seems like a nice girl."

"I don't know, Dad," I mumbled, reaching up to rub at the back of my neck. "We'll see."

* * *

Chloe Stephens, as it turned out, was persistent.

She came around the following Saturday, Baxter in tow, and rang our doorbell three quick times in succession right around noon. Given that it was a Saturday and my dad was in his office, oblivious to the world around him, I was forced to stumble out of bed and zombie-walk my way downstairs to the front door.

It hadn't even occurred to me that it'd be Chloe at the door, mostly because I was still half-asleep and hadn't really been doing any thinking at all. But as it was, I leaned forward to open the door, my hair a mess, my eyelids droopy, my body barely covered by shorts and a tank top, and then found myself face to face with her on the other side.

Both of her eyebrows shot up at the sight of me, and I was suddenly wide awake. And beyond embarrassed. She looked really cute in her pink V-neck, cut-off jean shorts, and navy blue Converse, and I looked like I belonged under a bridge.

21

"Whoa," she said at last, speaking first. I could see her trying to fight off an amused grin. "Not a morning person?"

I blinked at her, silently hoping my cheeks didn't look as hot as they felt. "Hi. Can you give me like two minutes?" I asked her.

"Sure."

"Okay. Thanks." I debated for a moment whether to invite her in or just leave her on my front porch, and, after an uncomfortable pause, I left the front door open, gestured awkwardly to the living room, mumbled that she could come in, and then left, taking the stairs two at a time back to my bedroom.

I changed quickly in front of my bathroom mirror and tried my best to clean myself up. Chloe probably didn't like girls, and I had no intention of developing an interest in her, given the number on her forehead, but she was still a cute girl, and cute girls made me self-conscious.

A few minutes later, I was headed back downstairs with my hair in a messy bun and with clothes on that were actually appropriate for the public: a long T-shirt and athletic shorts. Chloe was in the living room. She'd shut the front door behind herself and was playing with Baxter on our living room couch. When she heard me coming, she took him into her arms and tried in vain to get him to settle down. Once it was clear he couldn't calm himself, she sighed and set him on the ground. As she straightened up, her gaze shifted to me and she smiled.

"So, hey," she said.

"Hey," I said, and we stood in silence for a long, uncomfortable moment. I made myself focus on her face instead of her forehead.

She cleared her throat before things could get too awkward, and then gestured to the front door. "Well, I just thought that since it was the weekend and you don't have to work, you'd maybe wanna take a walk with Baxter and me? I don't really know the area. If your offer still stands, I mean."

"Okay." I nodded, feeling flustered. It seemed like the longer I stood in her presence, the more nervous I became. It'd been a while since I'd had any sort of extensive social interaction with someone other than Dad or Robbie, let alone a pretty girl. "Just let me tell my dad I'm going out."

I left in a hurry, my cheeks mildly hot, and burst into my dad's office. It was starting to sink in that Chloe had shown up at my house unannounced twice now, asking for my company. She was *really* set on spending time with me, which either meant that she was desperate to make a friend... or something more. I didn't have much of an ego, so I assumed the former, but both options were still terrifying.

"Give me an excuse to stay home. Please?" came bursting out of me before I could think about it. Dad spun around in his chair, an eyebrow already arched in questioning amusement. "I'm too nervous to do this."

"Is your friend back again?" he guessed.

"She's not my friend."

"Well, it seems like she wants to be." I pursed my lips together, and his amusement only grew. He spun away from me, facing his computer again, and casually tossed out, "Have fun. Be back before dinnertime."

"She could be a serial killer. Or the bait for a serial killer."

"Then I will miss you dearly. Goodbye, Harper."

I let out a sigh and spun on my heel, marching out of his office. By the time I was back with Chloe in the living room, I'd plastered a polite smile onto my face and the color had drained from my cheeks. She was cooing at Baxter, distracted, and gave a small start at the sound of my voice.

"Dad says I have to be back before dinnertime."

She recovered, reddening slightly, and smiled. "Cool."

* * *

I took her around the neighborhood first. We walked quickly to keep up with Baxter, who pulled heavily at the leash in Chloe's hand and refused to let her rein him in.

"So what do you do for fun around here?" she asked. "I bet there's a lot to keep you busy."

I realized pretty quickly that I wasn't going to make the best tour guide. "Oh, uh... I mostly just stay pretty local. There's a movie theater down the street, near where I work. And Robbie's got this place he really likes a couple miles away; it's basically a video game arcade with a whole special section for laser tag. They also have really good pizza." I felt like a dork as soon as I was done talking. Laser tag? Video games?

"Is Robbie your boyfriend?" she surprised me by asking. I laughed.

"Oh. No. He's, like, twenty-two."

"Ooh, an older boy." She grinned at me. "What's he like?"

"He's not my boyfriend," I insisted, and she laughed at my reddening face. "Seriously. He works with me; he's a cook at this fast food place where I work the register. He's a great guy, but... not my type."

"Because of the age or the geekiness?" she teased.

"I don't know." I avoided the question, shrugging. "He just isn't." I changed the subject. "So what do you wanna know about San Francisco? What are you into? Art? Music?" Glancing to Baxter, I added, "Animals?"

"All of the above. And I've never tried laser tag, but I bet I could be into it. I just wanna see everything. I've wanted to live here for so long."

I remembered she'd said that on the day we'd met, too. "Why?"

She shrugged, but I could tell she was the one avoiding my question now. "It just always looked fun and sunny and free. I grew up watching a lot of *Full House*. I don't know."

"Ah." I nodded, feigning understanding. "I

watched a lot of *Spongebob Squarepants* as a kid. Must be why I have this strange urge to live in a pineapple under the sea."

She shot me a look, biting on her lip to hold back a smile, and I was momentarily pleased with myself. "Very funny. I just wanted to, okay?"

We reached the end of the street that led to the front of the neighborhood, and I glanced up and down the street. "Hmm. If we take a left here, the movie theater's about a mile up the road. We can't take Baxter inside, but we could grab, like, tiny five-dollar ice cream cones from the concession stands inside. Or, alternatively, we could take a right and risk our lives when the sidewalk dead-ends in about five-hundred yards or so."

"So my options are death or inhumanely expensive ice cream?" She frowned. "Alright. Ice cream it is. But only 'cause I brought money and you're pretty." My lips parted in surprise as she veered left and let Baxter tug her along down the sidewalk. She glanced back at me and winked, then called back, "Are you coming, or do you have a boyfriend you should be with right now?"

She turned around and continued on without waiting on my response, and I glanced down to her left arm; the one not outstretched and gripping Baxter's leash. It hung at her side, swinging with every step she took, and as my gaze reached her forearm, I saw what I'd missed when I'd first taken in her appearance at my front door: a thin handmade bracelet encircled her wrist, repeatedly bearing, in order, the six colors of the rainbow.

I blinked a few times, sure I was imagining things. And then, when I was finally done and the bracelet hadn't vanished, I swallowed hard.

This was going to be a long summer.

Chapter Three

Once we had our ice cream, we sat together at a picnic table outside a restaurant next to the movie theater. Chloe licked at her chocolate cone and I tried not to stare as she declared, "You can totally tell a lot about a person by the ice cream they like." She eyed the vanilla cone in my hand judgmentally. "I have this theory that people who like vanilla ice cream are super safe and unadventurous."

I had no idea what to say to that. I was just allergic to chocolate. At last, I settled on, "Oh. I'm sorry to disappoint you...?"

"I forgive you. Would you ever go skydiving?"

"No," I answered instinctively, cringing at the thought of my parachute failing. She grinned.

"See? I'm right."

"What, you would?"

She nodded. "Of course. In fact, my dad says he'll take me soon. I'm a total adrenaline junkie. My parents took me bungee-jumping once when I was ten and it was amazing."

"Your parents trusted a springy cord with your life when you were *ten*?" I asked, appalled.

"I think the professional bungee-jumper that helped us might've taken some of the responsibility," she joked. "But yeah, my parents are pretty awesome. They're super into, like, the whole living your life to the fullest thing. They watch a lot of 'inspirational' documentaries, which is totally cheesy, but I can appreciate the sentiment. We've lived in six different states and two different countries since I was born. We've gone on vacations to Europe every summer up until this one, and my dad's got this long bucket list with every roller coaster he wants to ride before he dies and—" She paused, cringing. "God, I sound really obnoxious and pretentious right now, don't I?"

"I'm just listening," I told her idly. "It sounds interesting, actually. My life's pretty boring."

"I don't believe that. You live *here*."

"San Fran's not that exciting if you don't let it be," I told her. "My dad and I have a routine, and we follow it. There's not that much to share, I guess."

"What about your mom; where's she?" she asked me curiously. I stiffened, and, thankfully, she picked up on it. She immediately looked mortified.

"Oh, God, I'm sorry, Harper. I wasn't thinking."

"It's okay," I said. There was a long silence as we

awkwardly finished our ice cream together. I wanted to move past it, but I didn't know what else to talk about. So I elaborated instead. "She, um... died in a car crash four years ago."

Chloe let out a deep sigh and bit at her lip. "That's awful; I'm so sorry. I need to think before I speak a little more often."

I knew that this particular topic of conversation wasn't exactly first hangout material, but Chloe was easy to talk to. She talked a lot; she was all energy and earnest pseudo-rambling, at least around me, and for a moment I could only attribute to temporary insanity, I guess I thought it'd be a good idea to open up to someone other than Robbie. Or maybe I just wanted to open up to *her*.

"We were really close. She went out to have dinner with a friend and just... never came back." I shook my head, gaining a sudden sense of clarity. This was way too much too soon. "Sorry. I shouldn't be talking about it."

"I wanted to be your friend," Chloe insisted. "You can talk about anything you want. Especially someone you love."

I offered her a weak smile, and then bent down to feed the remnants of my cone to Baxter. "Thanks. It's okay, though. What's your favorite movie?"

She studied me carefully, and I kept my expression neutral. "You sure?" she asked.

"C'mon." I reached out to nudge her hand with mine, and her eyes jumped to the contact. I felt embarrassed that I'd opened up to her about my mom. Sure, Chloe was nice, but that didn't exactly make it natural to start discussing my dead mother the first time we hung out together. Especially given that hanging out with her was almost certainly an awful idea in the first place.

I could tell she was still stuck on the subject, so I reached out with my index finger and ran it along her pinky before withdrawing my hand. Her eyes flew to mine and, almost microscopically, her eyebrow rose in a silent question. I cleared my throat uncomfortably, already regretting touching her at all, and then repeated, "Favorite movie?"

She blinked twice, and then, to her credit, recovered quickly. "*Charlie's Angels.*"

I laughed despite myself, caught off-guard. "No it's not!"

"Drew Barrymore, Lucy Liu, and Cameron Diaz beating up bad guys? What more could I want?"

"Fair enough. Okay. Your turn."

"My turn to what?"

"Ask me something," I insisted.

"Like what?"

"Like... my favorite food, favorite color. I don't know. Anything."

"Okay. Let me think." She furrowed her eyebrows, staring hard at me for a moment and then, straight-faced, declared, "Your hair's in like a super messy bun right now, but it looks amazing. How do you do that? Seriously. I look like an ogre if I don't spend half an hour in front of the mirror."

I laughed at her and turned my nose up. "That

secret stays with me."

"No! Please? I'm jealous."

I felt a flush creeping up my cheeks and saw her grin. She knew she was making me nervous. That only made me *more* nervous. "Thanks," I mumbled.

"No problem, Harper," she said. That sly, amused look from the day I met her was back. My gut told me the way she was looking at me was a good thing, even if my head disagreed. "Okay." She cleared her throat and wrapped the remnants of her cone up into a napkin. "A real question: where do you work?"

I forced a laugh. "God. It's this fast food place called 'Daily Fries'. It sucks. We serve clogged arteries on buns, pretty much. I mean, I'm all for high-calorie, tasty food, but the stuff *we* make is toxic."

"You hate your job?"

"Loathe it, ugh." I wrinkled my nose and shook my head. "Who *likes* working in the fast food industry?"

"Why don't you quit?" She asked the question like she genuinely didn't know the answer. I thought it was obvious.

"Because I need the money. My dad wants me to start saving up for when I go off to college. I can't quit."

"Well, you could get a job you like," she suggested.

"It's not that simple."

"It could be. You won't know unless you try."

I laughed and joked, "Can you sew that inspirational quote onto a pillow for me so I can look at it every day before I wake up?"

She pressed her lips together like she was trying not to laugh and then tossed her balled up napkin at me with a pouty, "Don't make fun of me."

I grinned a grin I couldn't make go away, and for another moment, I forgot what I knew about Chloe's fate. That was something no one had ever managed before. It'd taken less than a couple of hours, but just like that, I was officially invested.

I should've aborted my idiotic non-plan right then and there, gone home, and saved myself the heartache. But something kept my brain from working properly and kept me there with her outside the theater.

Maybe it was the same omniscient power that had given Chloe her number. Maybe, just like there wasn't a way to stop the numbers, there also wasn't a way for me to come to my senses and leave Chloe alone.

At least, if there *was*... I'd spend months struggling to find it.

* * *

I'd always imagined that my first real crush would be like it was in the old movies my dad and I watched together. Love was Robert Walker as soldier Joe Allen running after Judy Garland's bus, calling out to her to meet him under a clock tower, or it was Julie Andrews and Christopher Plummer swaying together in the moonlight, or Claudette Colbert tearfully telling Clark Gable that she couldn't live without him. It was foreign: unattainable. I mean, I couldn't really even let myself get close enough to a girl to start to like her as a *person*, let alone as a friend or anything more.

Chloe shattered that image with a smile and a laugh, and after just a day together, I was wondering why I'd chosen now to let my guard down. Maybe a part of me really liked the attention: the way she was obvious about wanting and enjoying my company. Probably a part of me really liked *her*, and liked the way she so clearly liked me back. Liked me *first* even, because it was fairly obvious after just a few conversations that she hadn't been so pushy about hanging out with me without a reason. When I watched romances or read stories, I inserted myself into the main character's dilemma. I was the piner: the one loving someone and waiting for them to love me back.

But this was real life. And in real life, I was the love interest.

Chloe was interested in trying out laser tag, as it turned out. I took her a week later. And although Robbie came along, I offered to pay for her, since she'd paid for ice cream the week before. She let me.

Even with Robbie there, it still felt like a date from the moment it began. Maybe it still was. We were two girls who liked girls, even if Chloe didn't know that I was gay, and she certainly didn't *mind* not knowing it, because she flirted with me anyway.

The night before we went out, she called me at ten o'clock. I paused *The Wizard of Oz* to answer my phone, surprised to see her name on the screen. We'd exchanged phone numbers after ice cream, but had only texted a few times since then. She always initiated contact, and I couldn't force myself to ignore her messages.

"Hello?" I wasn't sure how casual I could be. We weren't really friends, and she was definitely more comfortable around me than I was around her.

"Hey, what are you up to?" she asked me. "Busy with your boyfriend?"

"This obsession has got to stop," I joked, taking a cue from her tone. "I can't tell if you're teasing me because you think I'm dating Robbie or teasing me because I'm *not* dating Robbie and therefore am single."

"Maybe it's both?"

"*The Wizard of Oz.*"

"Huh?"

"That's what I'm watching. *The Wizard of Oz.*"

"Oh. That witch terrified me as a kid." I heard a crunch on the line, and furrowed my eyebrows.

"What are you doing?"

"Eating a carrot. Gotta make sure my vision's at its best for laser tag, obviously."

"So you like carrots," I observed. "Mental note taken."

She laughed. "What, just in case you need ideas for birthday presents?"

"No," was all I said. I didn't want to think about

when her birthday was. I didn't want to know at all.

"So what kind of movies do *you* like? I've seen a lot of action flicks, but only because I mostly hung around guys back where I used to live."

I shifted my phone to my other ear as she bit down on another carrot. Then, before I could stop myself, I declared, "You're gay."

The crunching stopped. There was a short pause. And then, "Was that a question?"

"I'm sorry."

"For... pointing out the obvious?"

"I don't think it was obvious," I half-lied.

"Sure it was. I've always wanted to live in San Francisco, and I wore a rainbow bracelet the other day."

"The true reason you moved here comes out," I joked, trying to ease some of the tension. She ran with it, mercifully.

"Ah, yes. I definitely got my parents to pack up and relocate just so I could pick up girls more easily. The new puppy is also a ploy. It reels them in, you see?"

"Makes sense." I nodded and smiled, though she couldn't see it. There was another pause, and then she cleared her throat.

"Alright. Well I was just bored, so I thought I'd call my new friend. We *are* still on for laser tag tomorrow, right?"

"If you really want to."

She groaned. "Oh my God, I do! I knew I shouldn't have worn pink on our walk. I'm totally a dork, I swear. I mean, I've never shot a laser gun before, but I'll learn. Do you want to invite your other 'friend'?"

My gut reaction was to say no. I didn't want Robbie there. But I also realized, deep down, why I didn't want Robbie there, and so I agreed. "Sure. I'll text him about it."

"Cool. Pick me up at two, right?"

"Right."

"And my little dog, too," she croaked. "Not really though. I was just quoting your movie. Sorry. I'm dumb. Okay, bye."

"Bye." I forced a laugh, and she hung up. Then I pressed the phone to my chest, squeezed my eyes shut, and let out the deepest sigh of my life, mentally cursing myself.

Robbie came over the next day about half an hour before I was due to pick up Chloe and hung out with my dad for a while, who seemed a little wary of him. I saw Robbie's eyes glance to my dad's forehead when they first greeted each other and was already expecting a comment on it once we were alone, especially given that we'd never explicitly discussed my dad's number before.

As we sat outside on the front porch and he smoked a cigarette, he told me, "You're lucky."

"In the grand scheme of things, probably not," I pointed out. "Neither of us is."

"That's true. But your dad will be around for a long time. And he seems like a cool guy."

"Yeah."

We sat in silence for a moment, and I coughed as the cigarette smoke invaded my lungs. Robbie apologized and scooted away from me. I could tell he was deep in thought, but didn't know what was on his mind until he spoke again.

"So what're you doing with this girl, Harper?"

I leaned forward and put my chin in my hands, sighing. "I don't know." I hesitated, and then added, "I think she might be interested in me."

"So you're using me as a buffer. I guessed as much. Why don't you just tell her you're not interested?"

"Because." I shook my head. "I don't know. Maybe I am." I paused, and then corrected, "No, I'm not. But only..."

"Because she's going to die soon?" I squeezed my eyes shut, and my heart dropped as he turned to look at me. Hearing it said aloud made it so much more real than it seemed in my head. It ripped me right out of my own little world, where Chloe and I were on track to become best friends with a mutual crush, and dropped me right back into a reality that had declared her dead in who-knew-how-many months.

I bit my lip and nodded, but I still couldn't help but doubt that reality. Chloe was so *alive* now. She wasn't sick. She wasn't depressed. She was a perfectly functioning human being who seemed to really enjoy living. It seemed so unlikely that she'd have less than twelve months left. "What if her number's wrong, Robbie?" I asked him, even though

I knew what his answer would be before he responded.

"The numbers are never wrong."

"I know. But... maybe hers could be. Maybe I could change it this time."

"That's not how fate works, Harper. If she were to die at sixteen and had never met you, then that was always going to be the way her life went. But since she met you and her number's sixteen, she was always *going* to meet you, and meeting you – as well as anything you do to her or with her – won't stop her from dying at sixteen. You can't make a decision that's already been made."

"For someone who claims to be an Atheist, you sure do sound religious when you talk about this stuff, you know," I told him.

"I don't base it on some religious predetermination by a God. I base it on my own personal time theory. This is the present for us, but that doesn't mean there isn't a present in the future. And in that future present, this is the past. The past can't change, so everything's already set in stone. Fate knows the future, so Fate knows its past, which is our present."

"That makes no sense, you pretentious idiot," I groaned out. He put out his cigarette and shrugged his shoulders.

"It's just a theory. But we haven't seen a number change, so I'm automatically more right than you are."

"Well, I hope that makes you feel better," I bit

out.

"Not at all. It makes me feel like shit, actually." He got to his feet. "Let's go meet your friend, okay?"

"Okay," I murmured, but I was dreading it now. When Robbie saw Chloe, her number would no longer be a message for my eyes only. It'd be a lot like how coming out had been. Sharing it with other people; saying it aloud... that made it exist in a world outside of my mind. That made it real.

We said goodbye to my dad before we left, and he seemed particularly interested in how long we'd be gone, which was unusual. But I was too worried about Robbie meeting Chloe to dwell on it. Having him confirm her number was bad enough, but what if he saw something more? Something I hadn't noticed? A slight limp in her step, a twitch in a muscle. Something that could somehow indicate she wasn't long for this world.

I hadn't spent much time with her yet, but she was so lighthearted and just... *normal*, and it was impossible to imagine her life would be cut short by anything other than a terrible accident, especially after her adrenaline junkie confession. But terrible accidents were much easier to prevent than medical anomalies. That was a comfort, albeit an extremely miniscule one.

Chloe's father answered the door with a knowing look in his eyes and spent a lot more time introducing himself to me than to Robbie. Robbie was an afterthought. Robbie wasn't the person Chloe'd come home raving about, and the knowledge that came with Kent Stephens's excited greeting and eager shake of my hand made my heart thud harder in my chest.

"It's nice to meet you," I managed to get out before Chloe appeared behind her father. She grinned at the sight of me and, instinctively, I smiled back.

"Nice to meet you too, Harper. You guys will be back before dinner, right?"

"Yes sir. I'm driving," I told him.

"She won't run me over this time, I swear." As if to remind me further of that particular mishap, Baxter started barking in the background while Chloe slipped past her father and out through the front door. Kent looked like he wanted to talk more, but with Baxter fighting to get outside to be with Chloe, he thought better of it and bid us a quick goodbye.

"You told him about that?" I asked her when he was gone.

"More in the context of Baxter's latest antic," she reassured me, and then turned to smile at Robbie. "Hi. You're Robbie?"

"Yes." Robbie's eyes were fixed to her forehead, and I shifted uncomfortably, willing him to just be normal. I could see the fleeting worry in his eyes and knew instinctively that he was thinking of his sister, and of how young she'd been when she'd died.

Chloe, I was beginning to notice, liked to take control of awkward situations. She bailed Robbie out with a quipped, "So how long have you two been dating?"

I scowled at her, and Robbie shot me a confused look.

"She's kidding," I explained.

"Not entirely! No way are you single. C'mon, you can tell me. If we're gonna be friends, you'll have to start being honest with me eventually." She raised an eyebrow at me, straight-faced, and I tried in vain to keep my scowl on and resist blushing yet again in her presence.

Robbie bumped my shoulder, abruptly startling me out of Chloe and I's staring contest. "If we get there before three o'clock, there's a discount. Laser tag's half price from noon to three."

"Sounds great," Chloe cut in before I could speak. "Let's go."

She left without waiting for a response, walking straight to the car with her purse swinging off of her shoulder. Robbie nudged me and, sounding far too empathetic, murmured, "She's not even trying to hide that she likes you."

I felt my heart twist in my chest and tried my best to forget what he'd said as I moved to climb back into my car.

* * *

The entrance to laser tag was off in the corner of the arcade and had small wisps of smoke leaking out of it. I'd done this a few times before. The room was large, maze-like, filled with smoke, and square-shaped, with several winding hallways connecting scattered open areas. The walls that enclosed the hallways were tall and impossible to see over, but the ones in the open areas were waist-high and could serve as barricades or hiding places. The entrance was in one corner of the room, and in each of the other three, there rested a slightly raised, base-like structure where players could hide out and scope for "enemies".

It was a slow day at the arcade, and so Robbie, Chloe, and I were suited up for a three-way free-for-all match.

"Go easy on me, guys," Chloe laughed as her vest was activated by a male employee. "I have no clue what I'm doing."

"We'll team up against Robbie," I joked.

"Fine with me," he said and then darted into the smoky room without further warning, leaving Chloe and I behind.

"You'll know you've been hit when your vest lights up and starts beeping," the man who'd been helping Chloe explained once she'd been strapped into her vest and handed a gun. "For that time, your gun won't work and you can't be shot again. But after fifteen seconds, the lights will turn off and you'll be back in play. We keep score out here. You guys have twenty minutes starting from when your friend ran inside. Have fun!"

"Sounds easy enough." She adjusted her vest and then smiled over at me. "See you inside!"

And then she was gone. I waited a moment,

turning my laser gun over in my hands, and then, when I was certain I'd given her enough time, rushed into the room.

It was hard to see anything, but I could already hear the sounds of rapid laser-fire. That had to be Robbie. A distant "Dammit!" from Chloe a moment later confirmed it, and I laughed loudly as I ducked around a corner and saw her standing in one of the open areas, her vest flashing and beeping wildly. She spun around, free hand on her hip and poised to chastise me for laughing at her, but I ducked behind the wall again as Robbie fired at me from somewhere in the open space.

"Run, Chloe!" I reminded her.

"Oh. Yeah. Thanks!"

Robbie chuckled as her footsteps faded. He sounded close. I peered around the wall again, keeping my torso and vest behind the wall, and squinted through the smoke. A shadow caught my eye near a short wall less than twenty feet away, and I mashed the trigger of my gun several times until Robbie's vest lit up. He murmured a curse and hurried away.

We continued like that for a while. Our laser tag match essentially became a competitive hunt for Chloe, who basically ran around like a chicken with her head cut off, vest flashing wildly during her fifteen-second cool downs. Occasionally Robbie and I would shoot at each other once Chloe had been hit and had wandered away from us, but that was rare.

I was sure our time would be up soon after my

tenth hit on Chloe and third on Robbie, and I was also relatively sure I was in the lead by exactly two shots. The winner got a fifty percent refund on their entry fee, so I was somewhat invested in beating Robbie.

He got a hit on Chloe while I was hiding in one of the corner bases, and I watched her come barreling in my direction, red lights flashing everywhere. I kept an eye out for Robbie behind her, gun poised, but he played it smart, probably guessing that I'd be looking for him to follow Chloe's beacon of red lights. I tried to mentally count up hits in my head, double-checking the scores. He was one down now, so as long as I kept a low profile and he didn't hunt down Chloe again, I was pretty sure I had the win.

I was kind of proud of the stunt I pulled next.

Chloe's lights stopped flashing at last, and I listened to the sound of her footsteps as she came closer, hiding safely in my little base again. And then I heard a second set of footsteps, quieter and smoother, coming from the opposite direction. Robbie'd doubled back around, and she was going to run straight into him any second now.

A voice came over the intercom in the room to announce, "One minute left, guys," and I used the opportunity to dart out, snatch Chloe by the arm just before she hurried by, and yank her into the corner with me. She stumbled into me, crushing me against the wall, and I winced as I heard her start firing wildly. The feedback from the intercom covered up her first few shots, but I wasn't totally confident we'd escaped Robbie's detection.

"Stop it!" I hissed, grabbing her arm and yanking it up into the air. She twisted around so that we were facing each other and, thankfully, listened to me. "Don't shoot me and I won't shoot you," I explained.

She looked mildly frustrated with me as she lowered her arm, gun hanging from her hand at her side now. "You choose now of all times to team up? How many times have you shot me?"

"More than Robbie," I explained proudly. "I think I'm up by one. I'm gonna win."

She scoffed, and I looked down at our bodies, suddenly aware of how close we were. Her face was so close to mine that I could feel her breath, and I could tell by the hitch in it that she'd just noticed our proximity too. I tried to readjust our positions, but she stopped me.

"Shh. He'll hear." She was right, and her smirk told me she knew it. My heart rate picked up as she leaned in close to my ear. Her breath tickled my cheek as she whispered, "I suck at laser tag, but this is a lot of fun. Next time we should lose the boy."

My heart hammered harder. If Robbie couldn't hear our whispers, I was sure he'd find us just by listening for the sound of my pulse.

Chloe leaned away and reached up to tug lightly at a strand of my hair, grinning at me. She bit her bottom lip in a way that looked practiced, drawing my eyes to the motion, and then grinned wider as she dropped the strand of my hair and moved to trace her index finger up along my jawline instead. Her touch was softer now. Her thumb skimmed across my cheek and my pulse quickened to a rate I was sure it'd never reached before. My back was pressed against the wall and she was pressed against me, so I wasn't sure I could leave her, and I wasn't sure if I wanted to. My gaze hooded, I glanced back down at her lips again. She moved closer, and our noses brushed. She was going to kiss me. I closed my eyes...

And then I was twelve. I was twelve, and I was at a hospital, watching through a large glass window as the nurse on the other side quickly moved to pull a curtain across. Behind her, a team of doctors and surgeons surrounded a table my mother rested on. She disappeared from view, shielded by the curtain, but I could hear the heart monitor beeping so quickly, at a pace I was sure my own pulse could never reach. I pressed my right hand against the glass and let out a sob as my dad gripped my left...

I opened my eyes and registered a new kind of beeping even as Chloe jerked back away from me, surprise registering on her face. Her vest was beeping and flashing red, and behind her stood Robbie, his gun poised and pointed at her. His face looked almost comically grim as he leaned to the side just slightly, pointed his gun at me, and pulled the trigger several times in succession. My vest lit up just before the voice came over the intercom again. "Alright, guys. Time's up. Close game; it was a one-point difference in the end. Come on out and check out your scores."

I looked from Robbie, who clearly knew exactly what he'd just happened upon, to Chloe, who was red-faced, embarrassed, and hadn't taken her eyes off of me. And then I moved quickly, brushing past the both of them and hurrying out of the maze.

"Harper!" Chloe called after me, but I ignored her. I burst out of the smoke, shrugged off my vest and returned my gun, but didn't glance at the scores. Instead, I went directly to the bag I'd brought, fished out my car key, and handed it to the very confused employee who'd been watching me the whole time.

"Give this to my friends," I told him.

And then I ran.

I sprinted all the way home on foot, over three hours earlier than I'd planned on leaving the arcade. I ran until my legs were sore and straining and until my throat was aching and dried up from panting and until my heart was thudding so hard it felt like it was trying to tear its way out of my chest.

I collapsed on the sidewalk at the entrance to my neighborhood twenty minutes later and pulled my knees up to my chest, struggling to get my breathing even. I buried my head between my knees and resisted the urge to vomit. The earth was spinning, and I had to squeeze my eyes shut to make it stop. With them closed, all I could see was the surgeon from four years ago, and his grim expression as he'd told my dad that my mom's injuries were too extensive. They'd done all they could. He was so sorry.

My ears rang as I blinked rapidly and forced my eyes open again. Then I scrambled to my feet, stumbled to the bushes by the stone sign that bore the name of my neighborhood, and coughed harshly into them, my stomach churning.

At last, I steadied myself, confident I wasn't going to throw up, and took a few deep breaths. The past week felt like a bad dream. I wished it *had* been a bad dream. I wished I had a different pair of eyes.

I pressed my palms into my eye sockets and bit back a frustrated scream. "She'll be fine," I forced myself to say. "She'll be fine, she'll be fine, she'll be fine."

It was easier to repeat a lie than to face how stupid it'd been to speak to Chloe in the first place, but I still didn't believe it for a second.

* * *

I finished my walk home slowly. I wanted to recover before I saw my dad. I wanted to be able to look him in the eyes and tell him that Robbie'd forgotten an errand he needed to run, and that we'd left early so he could get it done this evening. I wanted to be able to say that it'd been a lot of fun and that Chloe was safely home and Robbie was in a hurry and was getting into his car as we spoke. And then I wanted to turn on an old movie with my dad and drown out the sound of Robbie pulling into the driveway with my car and then taking the hint and leaving in his without saying goodbye.

I wanted all of that, and I got none of it.

Robbie and Chloe, as I'd expected, didn't immediately assume I'd run straight home, and so I beat them back. That was what I'd hoped for, and I was relieved that I could put off talking to either of them about what'd happened back in the arcade. Their absence meant that I could bury my phone in the bottom of my purse and ignore their messages until Monday, in Robbie's case, and potentially forever, in Chloe's.

I knew I looked sweaty, but I could attribute that to nearly half an hour of laser tag. So that was okay, too.

What wasn't okay – or wasn't expected, at least – was that there was a car I'd never seen before in our driveway. It was parked next to Robbie's, and it was a red four-door. A car fit for someone closer to my dad's age than mine. A car I was certain I'd never seen before.

I fumbled for my keys as I walked up to front door, just in case it was unlocked. It wasn't. I opened it quickly, already trying to double-check my explanation to make sure it was usable in front of a formal guest. Dad worked from home, but he still had coworkers. Maybe a simple conference call wasn't enough for whatever he was working on at the moment.

"Dad?" I called out as I entered the living room, and my eyes fell to the couch. Dad shifted hastily, detaching himself from the woman sitting with him and running an anxious hand through his hair. But it was too late. I'd seen them, and I was staring now. They'd been kissing.

The woman turned to look at me, eyes wide with surprise. But she recovered quickly and offered me a shy, vaguely embarrassed smile. "Oh, is this Harper? I've heard so much about you!"

My dad and I were having a silent conversation of our own as she spoke. I swallowed hard, my whole body tense, and he shot me a pained look, still rubbing at his head. "Harper-"

I turned swiftly and hurried out of the room, taking the stairs two at a time as he called after me. I threw open my bedroom door and then slammed it shut behind me once I was alone inside. I locked it and then turned away, pressing my back up against the door. And before I could even register what I'd felt, seeing the two of them together, tears were streaming down my cheeks, and I couldn't prevent them from coming.

Eventually, I stopped trying.

Chapter Four

Dad tried several times to come talk to me, but I stayed shut up in my room for the rest of the day, buried beneath the piles of blankets on my bed. I kept my phone on my nightstand, turned on, and spent my evening listening to the buzzes of new text messages, or else to the sound of my ringtone as presumably Robbie or Chloe tried to call me. Dad came by at one point to talk through the door about what had gone wrong today at the arcade rather than what'd happened when I'd gotten home, so it was obvious Robbie'd reported back to him rather than letting me off the hook. I was eager to put off dealing with it, so I didn't respond to my dad.

I cracked first for Robbie, when he called me shortly after midnight. He sighed with relief when I answered him, a dull "hello" my only greeting.

"I was worried about you," he told me.

"I'm perfect," I deadpanned. "You can stop calling."

There was a long silence. At last, he told me, "Chloe was really upset."

"I don't care," I mumbled. "I hardly know her."

"Yeah, you do care. You like her."

"I hardly know her," I repeated.

"You still like her." When I didn't argue, he added, treading carefully, "It's okay to like her, you know."

I rolled my eyes. "You're so full of shit. You're the one who told me to stay away from her in the first place."

"That was my advice. It doesn't mean not taking it makes you wrong. I get it, okay? I get it better than anyone. Sometimes your head and your heart don't say the same thing."

"Look, it's not like I'm in love with her. We just met. I can just... tell her I'm not interested. Tell her to leave me alone. I never have to speak to her again, and then when she..." I trailed off, swallowing hard, and couldn't bring myself to say it. Instead, I let out a shaky breath and admitted, "She was going to kiss me."

"I know. I saw. I stopped it." He was silent for a moment. "Maybe I shouldn't have."

I didn't know what to say to that. I set the phone down on my bedspread and put him on speaker, then placed my chin in my hands. "My dad's seeing someone," I told him.

"I know. She was here when I pulled up."

"How can he do that? He didn't even tell me about her."

"Well, maybe he was worried that this was how you'd react." He seemed to hesitate for a moment before continuing. "It *has* been four years since your mom, you know?"

"That shouldn't matter."

"Of course it does. People move on, Harper. He loved your mom, but I bet she'd want him to be happy."

"You don't know anything about my mom or what she'd want," I bit out, and he fell silent. I rubbed at my face until I was sure my cheeks were red.

"That's true," he said at last, "but that's the way life works. You like Chloe now, but if you were to date her, you'd want to eventually date again after she was dead, wouldn't you?"

"Why do you have to be such an insensitive asshole?" I snapped, cheeks flaming, and quickly hung up on him. Then I threw my phone across the room and watched it hit the wall with a satisfying smack, where it broke apart into several pieces.

Breathing hard, I lay back down, pulled my covers over my head, and willed myself to wake up to a different world in the morning. One where Robbie wasn't so cynical and straightforward and my dad cared about my mom and Chloe didn't have less than a year to live. But that wasn't going to happen.

Chloe didn't know *anyone* in San Francisco. She had no friends. And she didn't deserve to die feeling alone in a new city.

I couldn't fall in love with her, I knew, but trying to help her was the only real option I had. I couldn't just ignore her now, and if I couldn't keep her alive, I could at least be there for her when she died. The last months of her life being happy ones were more important than anything I'd go through while helping make them happy. That was the right thing to do, even if it would be hard.

And besides: maybe, by some miracle, I'd do something to keep her alive in the process.

* * *

I answered Dad's sixth knock on my door around noon the next day, when I was finally somewhat prepared to hear him out. I was *so* angry at him – angrier than I'd ever been at anyone before, in fact. He'd given me that big speech at dinner all those nights ago about not regretting one minute of his relationship with Mom, but with the way his date had talked about me last night, it seemed like he'd been seeing her without telling me for a while now.

I understood loving someone and then loving someone else later. But Mom had been everything to me and him before she died. Four years had passed, but it felt too soon. Maybe it always would.

He didn't bring up last night when I opened my bedroom door. Instead, unable to look me in the eyes, he told me, "You have a visitor at the front door, honey."

"You sure it isn't for you?" I bit out as I brushed past him. He stiffened and didn't respond.

I was so busy trying to rile my dad up that I hadn't actually considered who my visitor was. Right around the time I reached the front door, I realized it was probably Chloe. I was ready to hear my *dad* out, but Chloe was a different story.

I paused, my hand on the knob of the front door. There wasn't really any turning back now. I exhaled heavily and pulled it open.

She looked up sharply and seemed surprised to see me standing there. In her hands was a sealed Tupperware container full of chocolate chip cookies, which she offered to me with a small, nervous smile and a proposal of, "Peace offering?"

"I'm allergic to chocolate," I told her, but accepted them anyway. "My dad will eat them, though."

"Oh, wow. That sucks. And explains the vanilla cone." She stood silently for a moment, chewing on her lip, and then seemed to collect herself. She shot me a pained look. "So... as it turns out, I sometimes do this thing where I flirt with a girl and then mistake discomfort due to lack of interest for discomfort due to nervous sexual tension, and then wind up trapping straight girls against walls and trying to make out with them. And then scaring the crap out of them and literally making them flee from me for several miles. On foot."

"Has this happened more than once?" I asked, dumbfounded.

She hesitated, and then admitted, "Well, no. You're kind of the only one. I have a pretty good gaydar. You don't have a boyfriend, you laugh at all my lame jokes, and I'm pretty sure you've actually spent more time blushing around me than *not* blushing around me so far. Turns out you're just kind of a nervous person, I guess."

I sighed, taking pity on her. "Yeah, I am. And also gay."

She furrowed her eyebrows, caught between looking thoughtful and inquisitive. "Well, now I'm confused. You didn't kiss me."

I arched an eyebrow. "Nice ego."

She flushed abruptly as her own words sank in. "I didn't... I mean... That came out wrong."

"I think it kinda came out how you meant it," I corrected, shooting her a sympathetic look and a smile.

"Okay. Maybe it did. I'm passably attractive and aware of it; sue me." She sighed, running a hand through her hair. "God, I shouldn't have come onto you during freaking laser tag. There are better ways to start out."

My smile faded. I set the cookies on an end table just inside by the front door, and then let out a sigh and leaned against the doorframe, my arms folded across my chest. Chloe'd relaxed now, and looked like she wanted to ask me to hang out for the day. "Chloe, I like you. But I think we should just be friends. I can't date you," I told her.

Her own smile faded. "...Oh?"

"I'm sorry." I bit at my lip. "I'm just not looking for a relationship." She opened her mouth and I added, "And I'm not looking for something casual, either. You're nice, okay? I want you around for a while."

She studied me for a moment, her mouth falling shut, and then, slowly, a smile tugged at the corners of her lips. "Okay. But I'm still going to flirt with you. Does this mean we can have sleepovers and pillow fights in our underwear?"

"You haven't had many female friends, have you?" I guessed, half-kidding.

"I used to call the girls that slept over at my house my friends back when I was in middle school. I'm not sure that counts, though. We probably got a little too friendly."

"Oh my God." I shook my head. "We are polar opposites. I have pretty much no experience with girls, *and* I'm older than you."

"That could change," she pointed out, winking. "And not much older, I bet, unless you're, like, eighteen. You're what, a senior next year? I just finished up my sophomore year, but I barely missed the cutoff to be in your grade; I'll be seventeen in August."

I'd realized what she was about to say just before she said it, but I wasn't quick enough at tuning her out. It took everything I had to keep a practiced smile on my face at the realization that she was only three months younger than me. August. She was turning seventeen in August.

That meant that Chloe didn't have twelve months to live. She didn't even have six.

She was going to be dead by the end of the summer.

* * *

Chloe left without coming inside after our conversation on the porch. I think she was more put off than she'd seemed by my rejection, and as I took the stairs up to my room, I wondered if I'd have been better off letting her think I was straight. Now the idea would always be in the back of both of our minds, even if I never let us actually go there.

I was upset with Robbie, but I knew I had to call him now. He was the only one I could talk to about Chloe.

I used my house phone, but he had the number saved and knew it was me. He seemed hesitant when he answered. "Harper?"

"Forget about last night," I told him. "I was pissed off and emotional. It doesn't matter anymore. Chloe turns seventeen in August."

He was silent for a long time. I picked at the comforter of my bed as I waited for his thoughts. "...How are you?" he asked at last.

"That's it?" I countered. "No advice? No telling me I should've known better?"

"It's not your fault you like her," he murmured. "Sometimes that stuff can't be helped. It happens. Against our better judgment."

"I guess." I let out a breath. "The only good thing

about this is that it has to be an accident. Right? I mean, barring the infinitesimally small chance that she has some rare brain tumor that's suddenly going to kill her, it has to be an accident."

"Another car accident," he mused quietly. I felt my heart clench in my chest.

"Well... I can watch out for that."

"How? By making sure she never uses a vehicle over the summer?"

"I don't know. I could drive her everywhere, maybe..."

"No," he cut in, so forcefully it startled me. "If it really will be a car accident, you shouldn't get into a car with her, Harper."

"Unless my age of death is 17, I think I'll be alright, Robbie."

"You can still get seriously injured," he reminded me.

"So if I can't stop an accident by driving her myself, how do I stop it?" I asked, realizing too late that his answer would be indicative of his usual philosophy.

"Harper, I don't think you can."

"I'm going to try," I insisted. "Even if I have to be her chauffer all summer and spend every hour of my spare time being with her and checking up on her." I set my jaw. "Everything I didn't and couldn't do for my mom."

Robbie didn't respond, but I knew what he was thinking. He didn't believe I could do it. I was determined to prove him wrong.

Later that day, Dad finally got to have the conversation he'd wanted. I initiated it by entering his office and offering him my SIM card. "Do you have an old cell phone I can put this in?"

He sighed and nodded, taking the card from me. Then he leaned back in his chair and folded his hands in his lap. "Harper, you know I love you dearly," he began, "but I think we both know that things have been different since your mother passed away. *I've* been different, particularly."

He paused, and I stared at him, waiting for him to go on. "Deborah and I met online a few months ago. She lives in the area, and her husband passed away in a fire a couple of years ago. He was a firefighter. Talking to her..." he trailed off, shaking his head. "Everything I'd been through, she'd been through. She could relate to it all. I haven't had that with anyone other than you." He shifted in his chair and looked to me pleadingly. "I think you'd really like her if you gave her a chance. A lot of the qualities I admire in her are ones I admired in your mother."

"She's not Mom," I reminded him gruffly. "She's never gonna be Mom."

"I know." He nodded. "I know. And when you were born, your mother and I promised each other that if anything were to happen to either of us, the other one would do the best job they could in raising you, and try as best as they could to be happy." He smiled proudly. "And I've done a damn good job with you. I love you so much, Harper. Now it's time for me to work on the other half of that promise."

I lowered my eyes to the ground, not sure what to say. "She's not a replacement?" I asked at last.

"Trust me. There is no replacing your mother," he told me, getting to his feet. "Okay?"

I looked up at him as he stretched his arms out for a hug, and then obliged him with a meek, "Okay."

As he hugged me, he explained, "I'm going to invite her over for dinner one night next weekend, okay? I think you'll like her, but if anything goes wrong, we'll talk it out, alright?"

I pulled away from him abruptly, eyebrows furrowed. Dinner with just me, Dad, and Deborah sounded like a train wreck waiting to happen. "Can I invite my friend? Chloe?" I asked him.

He didn't take too long to think about it before he nodded. "That sounds fair. Sure."

* * *

I consumed myself with Chloe for the next week. I made lists. Charts. Learned where she liked to go, what her schedule was like. It was borderline stalking, only she had no problem letting me do it. We developed a routine: every weekday, I'd get home from work late in the afternoon and then she'd come over. Depending on whether or not Baxter was with her and whether or not we felt like going out, we'd either hang out at my place or I'd drive us around. Chloe complained about my driving now; she said I was way too slow and way too careful, even when I was going the speed limit. I ignored her.

One of my lists – the most morbid – contained possible causes of death. I added to it every chance I got. An accident involving a vehicle was the most obvious cause, and it was right up at the top of the list. The lower down I went, the most ridiculous they got. It ended with "sky-diving accident" and then "random tumor," but I wound up crossing the second one out when I decided that the list should only be comprised of preventable causes.

Chloe's life became more than just an extension of my own. I buried myself in it with an enthusiasm I'd only had once before: four years ago. As the days passed, I could see the similarities cropping up in my subconscious: trouble sleeping and panicky episodes, for example. But I couldn't let up. Couldn't *give* up. I had to keep her safe. Had to keep Chloe safe. Had to keep *Mom* safe…

I was twelve. I was twelve and Mom was coming downstairs, dressed up for dinner with a friend. And while Dad was telling her how beautiful she looked, a feeling so powerfully foreboding settled within me that I felt paralyzed with fear. I watched her and Dad laugh together as he twirled her around, watching her dress spin, and then I blurted out, "I don't feel good."

They both turned toward me, and I tipped forward abruptly, and, barely managing to stay on my feet, vomited. They rushed to me, one on either side of me, and Mom held back my hair as Dad helped me stay on my feet.

"Honey, let's get you to your bed," Mom cooed in my ear. *"We'll get you a trash can to put beside it. Your dad will take good care of you."*

I shook my head and gripped at her. "No. I want you to stay."

She looked at me grimly. "I can't, sweetie. I have dinner plans with Pam."

"Please." I didn't know why I needed her around so suddenly, but the feeling was there, deep inside me, and I felt it from the top of my head to the tips of my toes. I couldn't ignore it. "Please stay."

"Your father will stay with you," she insisted, kissing the top of my head. "Let's get you upstairs."

I jolted awake, breathing hard, and fumbled for the clock on my nightstand. I turned it toward me and squinted. It was two in the morning.

Sighing, I rolled over and stared at my bedroom wall, vivid images from my dream swirling around in my mind. I didn't need time to recall the details; they were all already embedded deep in my head. That night was impossible to forget. I hadn't pushed hard enough. I'd known her number, and I'd had a feeling so strong it'd made me sick. But I hadn't pushed hard enough to make her stay.

If it happened with Chloe... *when* it happened with Chloe... I'd be ready.

Chapter Five

"So what you're saying is that I'm basically going to be forced to sit through the awkwardness along with you, then."

"Basically," I agreed, nodding over at Chloe. She grinned at me from the passenger's seat of the car.

"Okay. But I'm staying over afterward." She let out a squeal as Baxter surprised her from the back seat, jumping into her lap and licking at her face.

"Careful, I'm driving," I reminded her.

"Super slowly. Where are we going? You should just tell me."

"To one of my favorite places in San Francisco," was all I said.

"Is it a gay bar? I hope it's not. I don't want to meet other girls."

"I'm flattered," I joked and ignored the way my

stomach flopped.

"I have this theory," Chloe began.

"You have a lot of theories."

She ignored me and continued, "-that if I hit on you relentlessly enough, you'll crack eventually. See, when guys do it, it's creepy and gross, but I'm female and adorable and you actually like hanging out with me, so it's okay."

"Is it?"

She nodded simply and proceeded to kiss Baxter over and over on his head. He licked at her mouth and she saw me pull a face. "You're just jealous he gets to kiss me and you don't."

"Uh huh." I pulled into a parking lot and Chloe tugged at Baxter's leash until he was under control. Then we got out of the car together. "Okay." I pointed to the woods nearby. "We're following that trail there for only about half a mile or so. My dad told me about this place a few years back. He and mom went here in high school on their first date."

"Are you serious? And you try to act like you don't like me," Chloe marveled, her mouth wide open.

"You wanted to see where I go for fun and which places I like around here," I insisted. "This is it."

"And it's a romantic dating spot your parents used to use. How convenient," she drawled, sauntering past me. Or... attempting to. Baxter pulling at his leash ruined it a little.

We wound our way down the trail for ten minutes or so before we came to my parents' hidden gem of a spot. Buried in the woods was a drop-off that led to a small body of water, distantly connected to the ocean. Up at the top of the cliff above the water's edge was where I liked best, but nearby, the land sloped down to the water's level, complete with a small beach, and it was easy to wade into the water from there.

"Whoa. Does anyone else know about this place?" Chloe asked me, already leading Baxter down the slope. "This is awesome! We have to bring bathing suits next time; I wanna try jumping off of that cliff."

"Robbie knows I like it here. And you can't jump from there," I warned her. "There are rocks below; it's really dangerous. You have to just get in from where you are now." I followed her down the slope, pointing out the rocks in question. A few jutted out just visibly from beneath the water, but there were more underneath. "You'd have to be pretty lucky to miss them all. The drop itself isn't too bad; it's the landing that's the problem."

She frowned. "That sucks."

"Gotta get your thrills somewhere else," I lamented, patting her on the shoulder. She unleashed Baxter and he leapt into the water, splashing the both of us. I sat down on the sand as we watched him swim, and after a moment, Chloe joined me, admiring our surroundings.

"This is really beautiful, Harper."

"Thanks." I didn't know what else to say, and we both fell silent. As Baxter paddled back and forth, I felt Chloe shift closer to me. She leaned over and surprised me by kissing me gently on the cheek, and then rested her head on my shoulder. It felt natural, and I didn't stop her. I didn't want to.

"I thought San Francisco was going to be this constant gay pride parade," she told me abruptly. "Like, hot lesbians everywhere. I've gotta say... this is better."

"A seventeen-year-old socially awkward virgin with a job at a fast food place. *And* I'm refusing to date you. You sure hit the jackpot," I joked.

"I must break you," she replied in what sounded like a Russian accent. I pulled away to shoot her a confused look, and she looked disappointed.

"*Rocky IV*? No? Doesn't ring a bell?"

"They kept going after the first one?"

She sighed deeply, shaking her head. "What do you even watch?"

"I like older movies," I explained. "*Casablanca, The Sound of Music-*"

"You're so deep!" she sighed out, pretending to swoon.

"Oh, come on. Like, what's so great about *Rocky IV*?"

"Sylvester Stallone punches shit!"

"You're such a dude."

"Well, the actors in your movies were probably all bigots. So there."

"Because Sylvester Stallone is such a paragon of love and acceptance. Whatever. Julie Andrews is a gift."

"She's the exception," Chloe conceded. "But still. I grew up on action movies the same way you grew up on your old-timey stuff. We'll have to swap sometime. Or maybe watch one of each when I stay over." She seemed excited by the idea. "Oh. I can show you the *Terminator* movies! Have you seen them? You know: 'I'll be back!'"

"That Schwarzenegger impression was abysmal. No, I haven't. I'm showing you *The Sound of Music* because I know you haven't seen it."

"Okay." She nodded, grinning. "Deal."

* * *

Dinner with Deborah went, honestly, as expected. I didn't learn much about her. She was overly polite and asked me about my interests, and tried too hard to forge some kind of bond between us. We didn't have very much in common from what I could tell; some of her favorite activities included going on hikes and running marathons. That wasn't anything like my dad at all either, so I couldn't see why he liked her so much. She seemed nice, sure, but I took everything she said and did with a grain of salt. She was trying to make me like her, so, naturally, I didn't exactly warm to her.

Chloe was more polite than usual, too. It was her first time really getting to know my dad. They got along better than Deborah and I did. In fact, most of the conversation over dinner consisted of just the two of them talking. I stayed quiet unless someone addressed me directly. Most of the time it was

Deborah, with a question like, "So do you play any sports?" ("No.") or "Are you excited for your senior year to start?" ("I guess. I don't know.") All in all, it wasn't fun.

Eventually, Dad made the mistake of asking Chloe if she had any college plans yet or if she knew what she wanted to do when she got older, and I felt like sinking down into my seat until I disappeared. I didn't want to hear about Chloe's hopes and dreams and plans for her life. Not until I could ensure her safety.

I wasn't sure exactly what her birth date was, but I assumed it was mid to late August, right around when school started back up. That meant I needed to put everything I had into keeping her safe for two more months. If we could get to her birthday, then maybe things could be different with us.

To be perfectly honest, I wanted them to be.

We put on her movie first in my bedroom when we finished dinner (*and* after I spent quite a while assuring my dad that Chloe and I were just friends), and, after about two hours of watching Arnold shoot his way through just about every obstacle placed in front of him, up to and including a small army of human beings, it was time for my movie.

I yawned and slid down on my bed once I'd finished setting the movie up. Chloe and I'd sat on my bed for the first movie, popcorn between us and our backs pressed up against my pillows, but now she set the bowl aside and laid down to join me. I wondered, as she moved closer and her hand brushed against mine, if she was confused by my behavior. She had to know that I already liked her, for all her teasing about convincing me to date her in the future. There was really no reason for things not to progress naturally between us; at least, not from her perspective.

From mine, there was only the escalated emotional involvement that came with dating someone. If I committed, it'd make it harder to lose her. And a large part of me was worried that despite my best efforts to prevent it, I would.

I glanced over at her to see her watching the movie with rapt attention. She'd moved the popcorn to her other side, and the hand that wasn't pressing up against mine every few seconds had a fistful of popcorn in it and was currently being raised to her mouth. I smiled as she tried and failed to fit the entire handful.

"Don't get popcorn all over my bed, loser."

"Don't stare at me when your favorite movie's on, Romeo," she bit back, unfazed. "So desperate. God."

I huffed and hid a smile as I shifted my head back toward the television, acutely aware of the position of her hand again. I wanted her to keep touching me. I wanted to forget what I knew about her and just be *normal*. I didn't want to have to spend my summer playing God.

On the screen, Liesl and Rolfe were dancing together to "Sixteen Going on Seventeen", which was more than a little morbid given the circumstances. Chloe ate another handful of popcorn and murmured, "This asshole. I bet he betrays her. He looks sketchy."

I was only half-listening to her. My gaze drifted down to where our hands were nearly touching, and I shifted mine to bring it closer to hers. Heart thudding hard in my chest, I reached out with my pinky to brush it up against hers. She reacted by pushing hers back against mine and then linking our pinkies together, and I heard her swallow another handful of popcorn.

"Look at his douchebag, dancing around," she muttered, eyes still on the screen, but her pinky squeezed mine tighter between us.

"Can I ask you something?" I questioned abruptly.

She glanced over at me. "Hmm? Yeah, sure. Go ahead."

I searched her face for a moment, my eyebrows furrowed. "Why are you so forward with girls? Aren't you ever afraid of rejection?"

She laughed and shook her head. "No. I used to get nervous. Then one day I decided that was stupid. So now, whenever I start to hesitate, I just tell myself to not worry about the consequences, push past the nerves, and do whatever it was I almost didn't."

"That seems like a good way to make a lot of mistakes," I pointed out.

"Life's all about mistakes. And it's way too short to just wait around instead of cutting through the bullshit."

I shifted backward to get a better look at her face. "Is that what this is? The bullshit?" I wasn't angry, and took care not to sound that way. I just genuinely wanted to get inside her head.

"Of course not. This is… me spending a summer with a pretty girl, who, if she were to decide she maybe did actually wanna act on her urge to kiss me, would be welcome to do so."

"You're waiting," I restated for her. "You just said life's too short to wait around."

"I make exceptions." She arched an eyebrow at me. "If you have a problem with it, you could end the waiting. Especially given that I'm not really sure what we're waiting for. I mean, it's been like three weeks since we met now. We live in San Francisco so homophobia won't be a problem. I'm solidly gay, and you're not exactly waving a rainbow flag but you *have* claimed to play for my team, so."

I didn't respond. We laid in silence for a moment, facing each other. I watched her lips part as she let out an overdramatic sigh and thought of Robbie and what he'd say about this. He'd probably make extra sure I knew that Chloe was doomed regardless, because fate had already made its decision. He'd also probably say that I was a lost cause. Maybe that was true.

Chloe chewed on her lip as we broke eye contact and her gaze drifted lower. Her hand came up and touched my cheek, then slid down to my neck and stayed there, her fingers unconsciously urging me forward by putting pressure at the base of my skull.

I watched her, unmoving, and swallowed hard. She'd stopped biting her lip and was smiling at me now, and I marveled at the fact that a girl like her could ever be interested in a girl like me. She lit up rooms when she walked into them, and I was the epitome of the shy, antisocial kid that sat alone in corners at parties. Yet here we were, her with her hand on my neck as she shifted ever so slightly closer.

"Why do you like me?" I asked her.

She looked confused by the question and backed off. "Because you're cute."

"No, seriously." I sat up, and her hand slid off of my neck as she joined me. I watched her, waiting.

She took a deep breath and then rolled her eyes. "Because you're *cute*." I opened my mouth to chastise her, but she kept talking. "That was the reason after we talked for the first time, anyway. After that... I don't know. You were interesting. You have so much going for you: a nice dad, your looks, the dry sense of humor." She smiled, almost sadly. "But it feels like... everything's grey to you."

"Grey?" I echoed, confused.

"Like the whole idea of going through life as we know it is just... 'meh'." She shrugged her shoulders. "You don't get excited about much. There's not a lot you like. Not a lot you do. It's like you don't have an enthusiasm for life. Which was interesting to me because I get excited about *everything*. Maybe I'm too enthusiastic; I don't know. But I think we could balance each other out.

You need a little color in your world, you know? Even most of your *movies* are in black and white."

"So I'm a charity case," I sighed out, only half-meaning it. "I get it."

"No." She straightened up and, with an air of false pretentiousness, declared, "I find you intriguing." Then she dropped the act and added, "And once I got vibes that you were a cute girl who could actually be a lesbian, there was no going back."

"It doesn't take much, then?" I joked.

"Well, who says it should?" She shrugged again. "I like you. It doesn't have to be complicated, and there doesn't have to be years of tension and buildup. I just met you and I like you and that's enough for me."

"Things aren't always that simple," I shot back, tensing.

She exhaled audibly, watching me, and then seemed to hesitate before she spoke next. Her tone was gentle, like she wanted to tread carefully. "Harper, I've only ever lost one family member, and it was when I was young, so I won't act like I know what that's like. But the only person I've seen you happy around has been Robbie. This is about your mom, isn't it?"

I hesitated. I felt frozen in place as I tried to come up with a fitting response, but she'd caught me off guard. My silence was a reply in its own right.

"I'm not going anywhere," she said, offering me a small smile. "It's okay to let people in sometimes."

"You promise?" I asked, even though I knew it wasn't fair."

"I promise."

"I-" I paused, hesitating again. She was so earnest: so sincere. She had no idea she wasn't telling the truth, and as I studied her, I couldn't help but think, *"What on earth is going to happen to you?"*

"Can I ask you something?" She spoke up suddenly. "Why Robbie? What is it about him that made it okay to keep him around?"

I shifted my gaze to my lap with a soft sigh. "Well, it helps that I'm not attracted to him. And... his sister died a few years back. He gets it. And... I just have a feeling he'll be around for a while."

"Doesn't that get exhausting?" she marveled. "Looking at every single person like some sort of risk calculation? Comparing potential enjoyment as a result of being friends versus potential pain as a result of losing the friendship? Or of losing *them*?"

"Yes. It's very exhausting." I shrugged. "I wish I wasn't like this, but I can't change it."

"I think you can. Have you ever considered the fact that maybe the goal of life isn't to get through it as painlessly as possible?" she asked me.

I raised my head, genuinely caught off guard again. "No, not really."

"Well, there you go. There's your problem. Life isn't about the pain. It's about the good parts. Think about it like... laser tag!" She brightened even as I forced a laugh. I could see the cheesy metaphor coming before she even began. "Like, I bet it'd be super easy to go a whole round without getting shot. You'd just have to hide in some corner where no one ever goes and sit there and do nothing. But that makes for a boring game of laser tag, and so no one does that, right? We all run around and put ourselves at risk so that maybe we'll have some fun! See, life is like laser tag."

I stared at her for a moment, trying to keep a straight face. "Uh huh."

"That was a fantastic metaphor. I came up with that literally just now; wasn't that awesome?"

"For an improvisation," I humored her. "The thing is, I know what it's like to get shot, and I've learned from it. I'm not letting it happen again. You've never been shot, so you don't know how bad it feels."

"I don't," she admitted, but she was smiling now. "But I *do* know how fun it is to not hide in a corner all game."

* * *

Dad was waiting for Chloe and me with breakfast when we came downstairs the next morning. He had enough tact, thankfully, to not ask about our sleepover or about what I'd thought of Deborah while Chloe was with us.

She left just before noon, and I walked her to the door. "I'll see you soon," she promised. "My parents want to see a movie with me tomorrow night, but I'm free every other night this week. I thought of something we might be able to do together next weekend."

"Oh no," I joked.

"It'll be fun," she insisted. "Trust me."

We stood together for a moment, face to face, and she looked like she wanted to say more.

"I'll see you around, then," I said.

She nodded. "Not going anywhere."

"I remember," I assured her. "Just... be careful. No skydiving before I see you again, okay?"

"I can't promise that," she joked. "Text me, alright?"

"Yep."

She leaned in before I could react and kissed me on the cheek, then took a couple steps back, grinning, before she turned away and descended the porch steps. I sighed and leaned against the doorframe, watching her go and, at last, turned to go inside and closed the front door behind me.

Dad was watching me from the living room, an eyebrow raised. I colored instantaneously and he asked, "Just friends, huh?"

"That looked worse than it was," I mumbled.

"I'll let you off the hook," he acquiesced, "if you tell me what you genuinely thought of Deborah last night."

I shrugged my shoulders. "Not much to think. She tried kind of hard, didn't she?"

"Because it's important to her that you approve." He folded his arms across his chest, looking concerned. "It's important to me, too."

"Well... maybe she and I are just meant to coexist," I suggested, turning away from him. "We don't have to be best friends."

He let out a sigh. "I didn't say you did, Harper. Just... promise me you'll give her a chance, alright? You hardly spoke to her last night."

"I'll give her a chance," I agreed quietly, and then mumbled, "It's not like I have much of a choice, anyway."

* * *

"Welcome to Daily Fries. What can I get for you?"

The man in front of me took his time with the menu on the wall. It was Three Burgers again, back for his daily meal with a 45 still on his forehead. I felt physical pain as I watched him speak. "*How are you this stupid?*" I wanted to ask. "*There are people who care about you and you're literally killing yourself.*"

He stopped speaking. Now he was staring at me. I realized I'd completely spaced out while I was supposed to be taking his order. "I'm sorry, sir, could you repeat that?"

"I just spent an entire minute giving you my order," he shot back, appalled. "You didn't get any of it?"

I bit my lip to stop myself from being rude. A hand on my shoulder saved me. Robbie, of course. He looked out for me far more than I deserved. "Sorry about that, sir. I'll take your order and we'll throw in a free large fry; how does that sound?" He

79

gave me a look that told me to scram, and I rolled my eyes and left to go on break.

When I was outside alone, I sat down on the ground, my back to the wall that was still covered in cigarette burns, and pulled my knees up to my chest. I rested my forehead on my knees and closed my eyes, willing my shift to be over soon. This was a waste of time. I could've been with Chloe all day instead.

Robbie came around a few minutes later. I heard his footsteps and the click of his lighter before he spoke, but when he did, it was with a sigh. "You could ask George if he'll give you the rest of the day off," he suggested.

I lifted my head to look up at him. "I'm thinking about quitting."

"Since when?"

"Since a few weeks ago," I admitted. "I hate it here."

"Well, no one *likes* it here."

"Yeah, but..." I trailed off and then muttered, "I hate being around people."

"Me too," he agreed quietly. "This job gets morbid sometimes."

"I need something where I never see anyone," I decided. "Like a data entry clerk job or something. With a desk in a back room. And the only person that ever comes in is my boss, who has super healthy eating habits and will live into his hundreds. I'm so sick of being reminded that we're all going to die one day."

"Well, hook me up when you find a job like that." He exhaled a cloud of smoke and I pressed my nose into my sleeve. "I'll tell George you aren't feeling well, okay? Go see Chloe."

"What's the point?" I mumbled, only half meaning it.

He studied me for a moment. The cigarette between his fingers slipped through them and fell to the ground, where he squashed it with his foot. "I'm a pretty cynical person. Even more cynical than you, which is saying something. So as much as I'm sure you don't want to hear it, here's the truth. All of this isn't going to end well. You fucked up pretty badly by putting yourself in the position you're in. If you hook up with her and she dies, you'll be miserable." He paused, digging the heel of his shoe into the gravel beneath us. "With that said... If you *don't* hook up with her and she dies, you'll be miserable *and* you'll regret it."

I hid my face against my knees and tried to ignore how low my heart had sank. "Maybe."

"Not 'maybe'. If I was wrong, you'd just stop spending time with her, because it wouldn't be worth it. Instead, she's the only thing that's been on your mind since you met her. I kind of miss you, actually."

I wiped at the corners of my eyes and couldn't bring myself to look back at him. "This sucks."

"I warned you about this happening." His tone was blunt. Typical tactless Robbie. I tried hard to not get mad at him.

"I think I'm gonna go. Can you talk to George for me?"

"Of course." He stood with me for a moment, and then, awkwardly, said, "I'm here if you want to talk."

"I know."

He hesitated, lingering for another few seconds before he left. I got to my feet as his footsteps faded, and my stomach twisted into a knot. Before Chloe, Robbie had been the only person who'd understood me.

Now it felt like no one did.

Chapter Six

"Hey, what's up?"

I tried to hide a sniffle, hoping Chloe couldn't hear it through the phone. "Um, are you busy?" I asked her.

"Just playing a board game with my parents. Why?" I didn't answer at first, and Chloe sounded concerned the next time she spoke. "Is something wrong?"

"Not really. I just... thought you might come over?"

"Sure. Just give me a few minutes and I'll be right there." There was a brief pause, and I heard what sounded like two distinct voices in the background. A moment later, Chloe was back on the line. "Hey, um, actually, how do you feel about coming here? If you don't want to, I can come over, but Dad's only met you that one time and Mom wants to meet you. We can provide free food..."

I considered it. Earlier on in my friendship with Chloe, I'd wanted to avoid her parents. But a few weeks had passed and things were different now. Getting to know her parents wouldn't make things much worse than they already were. It was probably worth it to make Chloe happy. Talking to her alone could wait.

"Okay."

"Seriously?" She sounded surprised. Apparently I'd been a little more obvious about my urge to keep away from her family than I'd originally thought. "Okay, awesome! See you soon?"

"Yes," I confirmed and hung up.

I went to the bathroom and looked at myself in the mirror. My hair was messy, my mascara was smeared, and I probably smelled like fast food. I did what I could to fix myself up, and was halfway out of the house when Dad stopped me.

"Where're you off to? I thought your stomach was bothering you."

"Um, I feel a little better now," I explained. "It stopped hurting. I'm just going to Chloe's."

He studied me, eyebrows furrowed. I could tell he didn't believe me. "Are you sure? You seemed pretty upset when you got home."

"I'm okay, Dad." I brushed a stay tendril of hair out of my face and turned away from him quickly, eager to go.

"Wait a second, Harper. What aren't you telling

me?"

I froze in the doorway and let out a quiet sigh. Then I faced him again. He'd folded his arms across his chest now. "It's nothing, Dad. Just... typical teenage girl stuff. I'm PMS-ing and a boy broke my heart."

"Very funny. I've known you your whole life; don't think I haven't realized that the biggest sign something's wrong with you is when you start using jokes to deflect my questions."

"I'm just going to Chloe's," I insisted. "I'm playing board games with her family. They're feeding me. I'm okay."

He watched me for another long moment, and then pressed his lips together almost sadly. "I worry about you, Harper."

"Yeah, I know. I'm anti-social. So keeping me from my new friend is definitely helping."

"You've been different lately," he told me. "You come home upset and don't tell me why, you broke your phone the other week; you don't tell me what's going on in your life-"

"Oh, that's rich coming from you." I rolled my eyes and mirrored his crossed arms with my own, the open front door abandoned behind me. "You had a girlfriend and didn't tell me."

"And given how you've reacted, can you blame me?" He shook his head, and I stared at him, suddenly feeling very numb. "It hasn't been easy with just the two of us, Harper. But we'd watch our shows and movies together and had nightly dinners and I always knew what was going on with you and what you were going through, even if I didn't understand it all. I always felt close to you. And now, out of nowhere, there's this wall up I can't get past and I can't figure out why. I feel like I've done something wrong."

He paused like he was waiting for a response, but I made no move to answer him. I just wanted to leave.

He deflated, and I watched him close his eyes and let out a deep sigh. When he spoke again, he sounded defeated. "I wanted to take us to do something fun this Saturday. Deborah likes to go camping and I thought maybe you'd want to join us. But I guess it would've been a mistake to ask."

There was a long silence as we stared at each other. I broke eye contact first.

My tone felt flat as I told him, "I'm going to Chloe's now," and I turned and left through the front door without waiting for an answer.

* * *

Chloe's dad was married to a woman named Hayley. She had Chloe's light blonde hair and bright blue eyes, and there was a softness to the way she spoke and smiled that reminded me painfully of my own mother. I thought her name fit well. They sounded like a family. Kent, Hayley, and Chloe. As I spent the evening watching television and playing games with them, I wondered why their family had to be the one to be broken. They were so obviously happy in a way I could no longer remember being.

"Chloe tells me you're joining us at Six Flags this weekend. It should be fun," Hayley told me over dinner. I looked at Chloe next to me, taken aback, and she sighed at her mother.

"*Mom!* That was supposed to be a surprise!"

"Oh! I'm sorry, honey. I thought you'd told her."

"Wait," I interrupted, raising both eyebrows at Chloe. "That was what you wanted to do this weekend?"

"Well, yes. If you were okay with it. Dad wants to check out the rides and I thought it'd be fun if you came along."

"I'm seriously not a fun person to take to amusement parks," I explained. "I can't ride half the rides because I'm a coward. *And* it's expensive."

"Oh, don't worry about that," Hayley cut in. "We'd be happy to have you along. Chloe can't wander around the park alone, anyway."

Faced with Hayley and Kent, who was nodding along beside his wife, I couldn't turn them down. "Wow. Thank you. I'll try not to be boring?"

Kent chuckled as Hayley's smile widened. "I'm sure Chloe'll keep you busy."

* * *

"Is your dad expecting you back soon?"

I shook my head and avoided Chloe's curious look at my response. We were up in her room and a couple of minutes had passed since we'd finished dinner. Chloe's bedroom was everything I'd expected it to be: a *Charlie's Angels* poster adorned one wall, and a poster advertising a Missy Peregrym movie hung on another, her abs on display. The walls were painted a darker beige color, but not so dark that it seemed dreary. Her bed was large enough to fit at least three people on it comfortably, and Baxter, too.

"I like your parents," I told her. I was poised on the edge of the bed, and Chloe laid across it on her back, tossing a small stuffed bear up into the air and catching it over and over again. Baxter lay on the floor beside us, fast asleep. It was the first time I'd ever seen him relaxed.

"Yeah, they're pretty awesome. They get a little too involved sometimes, though, which can get annoying."

"I like that. It means they care."

"I guess so." She caught the bear and looked over at me, a hint of a smile on her lips. "They think we're hooking up in here."

I wrinkled my nose and feigned disgust. "Gross."

"Shut up!" She tossed the bear at me, and I deflected it with one hand, grinning. "I didn't tell them anything, just so you know. I just haven't known you for more than a month and I guess I already don't shut up about you."

"That's quite the accomplishment given that I'm pretty boring," I told her. She sat up with a scoff.

"No, you're not. I refuse to have a boring best friend."

The label was unexpected, and it warmed my

insides. I didn't say anything, and she arched an eyebrow at me.

"What? Am I moving too fast? Is it too soon to stop pretending like I hang out with anyone else *other* than you?"

"What about before here? You must've had friends where you used to live."

She shrugged her shoulders. "Yeah, well... you know how it is when you move."

"Actually, I don't. I've lived here my whole life."

She went back to lying down, her lips pressed together and her fingers interlocked over her stomach. For a moment, she looked deep in thought. Then she said, turning back to me, "I guess I had a lot of acquaintances. There are people you know and then people that *know* you, you know?"

I grinned at her. "Can you repeat that?"

"Okay," she huffed out. "It's like... I had a lot of people who knew my name and said 'hi' to me when we'd cross paths in the hallway at school or whatever. If I had a birthday party, I could get people to come. But I've never had the kind of friend I could just spill my guts to and feel comfortable with it. That feels natural with you. Maybe because it doesn't feel like you judge me. Anyway, what I'm trying to say is basically that high school sucks."

I forced a laugh and watched Chloe close her eyes. She seemed to relax in front of me, and I almost felt guilty when I finally broke our silence. "I can't remember the last time I had a friend my own age."

Her eyes fluttered open and she smiled over at me. "Well, now you've got me... And you're *so* riding coasters with me this Saturday."

"Ugh," I groaned, flopping down next to her. "Great. And right after that I can meet up with Dad for the most awkward camping trip of my life."

"What, with the new girlfriend?"

I rolled my eyes at the ceiling. "Dad said she likes to camp, and right before I came here, he stopped me and got all mad at me because I'm not making an effort with her. She's not *my* girlfriend."

"I bet it'd make him happy if you went." Chloe sat up beside me as she spoke, and I frowned over at her.

"Why can't you just tell me that he's a jerk for hiding her from me and that I totally have the right to be angry about it?"

"He's a jerk for hiding her from you and you totally have the right to be angry about it," she recited. "Also, I still bet it'd make him happy if you went camping with them." She perked up and nudged me. "Ask him to bring me! Use the Six Flags trip to make him feel guilty. I'm treating you to a free day at a theme park. It'll totally work."

"That's so manipulative." I pondered the idea. "I like it. You sure you want to sacrifice a night in this amazing bed, though?"

"I can sleep in this any night. I'll keep you company," she insisted. "It'll be fun. We're can spend most of the day at the park, and then we'll be so exhausted we'll pass out before it even sinks in that we're sleeping in a tent. Oh, but before that we can make s'mores!"

"Chocolate allergy," I reminded her, and she groaned even as the words left my lips.

"How do you *live*?"

"Like Voldemort. A half-life. A cursed life."

She snorted, and then her eyes widened and she hid her face, embarrassed. I laughed at her openly.

"You do that sometimes."

"Don't make fun of me! It's my one flaw."

"Aw, no. I think it's cute," I insisted, trying to make her feel better. When it actually occurred to me what I'd said, I pressed my lips together, regretting it. Chloe turned to look at me even as she brushed her hair out of her face, and I could tell she was struggling to hide a smirk.

"Oops," was all she said, the teasing smile finally breaking free, and I rolled my eyes and bumped her shoulder with mine, playing it off and hoping I wasn't turning red.

"Yeah, whatever."

"So what else did your dad say before you came here?" she asked me abruptly. "You sounded upset on the phone."

"Oh that wasn't about-" I started to say, and then realized that I couldn't tell her about what'd happened at work, given that she'd been the cause of it all. I changed gears and said instead, "...about the camping thing. I guess he thinks I'm not as close to him as we used to be. I don't know. This summer's just been stressful with work and..."

I trailed off, and Chloe finished, "Me?"

I avoided her eyes, embarrassed she'd been forward enough to make the suggestion. I shrugged. "I guess." I paused for a moment to collect my thoughts and was thankful that she didn't interrupt me. "I guess maybe I just feel like I can only handle so many people at once. Dad's got this whole thing with Deborah going on, and Robbie and I haven't been talking as much, and I hate my job, but I don't know if I can afford college without it, and... now there's you."

There was a long pause and I felt more and more embarrassed the longer my words hung in the air. At last, Chloe said, her tone brighter and more matter-of-fact than I expected, "I get it."

"How?" I shot back, eyes on my lap. "Your parents are together and they seem really cool and they get along with you, and you're not working, and you don't have a Robbie that likes to randomly remind you of how hopeless and meaningless life is in the long run. Every time I even get near him I have an existential crisis."

Another long moment passed where neither of us spoke. Eventually, Chloe turned to look at me, eyebrows furrowed, and asked, "Is Robbie a stoner?"

I let out a small laugh purely out of surprise. "Uh, yeah."

"So doesn't he spend his spare time smoking weed and contemplating the meaning of life while staring up at the stars? And then the next day he'll spend the whole work shift mumbling about how we're all ants or cogs in the machine and in the long run we're not going to make any difference in the world?"

I chuckled and nodded, raising a hand to cover my mouth. "Oh my God. That is almost eerily spot-on."

"Yeah, that's not the best guy to be taking life advice from. I mean, I'm sure he's a smart guy, but I've known guys like that and they'll make you depressed as hell. Especially if they're jaded."

My smile faded and I turned away from her. "Well, I don't know if I'd call him 'jaded' because he lost his sister..."

She winced beside me. "Shit. I didn't mean it like that. I'm sorry; please forget I said it." She hesitated before she continued, and I could feel her gaze on my cheek. "If I lost someone I cared about, I'd probably spend a lot of time wondering why things are the way they are, too. I understand. I just... wanted to make you feel better, I guess. I thought making a joke about it-"

"It's okay," I cut her off before she could start rambling. I looked back at her to see her relax a little. "I know. Sometimes he pisses me off. But sometimes he's the only person who makes sense. Or the only person who says the right things." I elbowed her lightly and cracked a smile. "But he also has his fair share of foot-in-mouth moments, too. And he's not as attractive as you."

She shook her head disapprovingly, and there

93

was a small, almost sad smile on her lips as she prodded my shoulder with her index finger. "Thanks, but don't hit on me, okay? The one slip-up was enough."

"But you're so pretty," I joked, and quickly stopped grinning when I realized she wasn't playing along. Instead, she nudged me again, her voice quiet.

"Harper, c'mon."

Now I was the one who felt awful. I didn't know what to say, so instead I just nodded and started to move off of her bed.

"Wait, you don't have to go," Chloe said. She looked surprised now. "I wasn't saying you had to go."

"No, it's okay," I replied, trying to keep my voice even. I couldn't make eye contact with her. "I should go talk to my Dad. He'll be happy to hear I want to go do the camping thing with him."

"Harper-"

"I'll see you later, okay?" I interrupted, and left quickly before she could follow.

* * *

At some point, I knew I had to face the way I felt about Chloe, and the fact that it was mutual. This wasn't a fairytale. This was a real person with real feelings, and even though I wasn't guaranteed a happy ending, a decision needed to be made.

I trembled as I helped Dad pack for our camping trip. When I was done, I'd go to Chloe's house and join her family for a late breakfast. Then we'd go to the theme park for the day, get home around six, and Chloe and I would go with my dad and Deborah to a campground Deborah had experience with. I wasn't sure which terrified me more: roller coasters, sleeping in a tent in an unfamiliar area, or the fact that I was doing both in one day with Chloe.

I packed painstakingly slowly. Robbie texted me through it. I wondered if he was nervous for me. Even if he didn't like to admit it, I knew I was his best friend. And I also knew that watching him go through what I was going through now wouldn't exactly be a cakewalk. Robbie and I'd had countless conversations about staying detached from people outside of our families, and yet here we were, attached to each other. But at least I knew Robbie was going to be around for a while.

I got my first moment of peace in a while on the way to the park. I'd grown afraid of car trips with Chloe, but with her mother and father in the car with us and both of them sporting high numbers on their foreheads, I had somewhat of a guarantee for the first time that there would be no car-related incidents today.

Chloe and I sat in the backseat, she behind her driving father and I behind her mother. I rested my head against the window and watched the trees on the side of the road blow past us. My hand, almost unconsciously, stretched out toward the center of the seat, occasionally making contact with Chloe's fingertips. Her doing. She'd made it clear the other night that as long as I was the one doing the rejecting, I wasn't allowed to also do the flirting. I supposed that was fair. I couldn't have it both ways.

I took my forehead off of the window and looked over at her. Her gaze was on the view of the body of water just a football field's distance from us, and when she used the hand that wasn't playing with mine to tuck a strand of hair behind her ear, I could see her smiling.

"This is beautiful," she murmured, awestruck. "Isn't it?"

Still staring at her, I had to work hard to avoid agreeing with her in the cheesiest, most cliché manner ever recorded by modern humanity. But 2000-era romance movies suddenly seemed less contrived and annoying.

Instead, I sighed and turned away, pressing my forehead to the glass window again. Then I pulled away and drove my head forward until my forehead met the glass again with a small "thunk".

It didn't help.

* * *

Despite spending all seventeen years of my life in San Francisco, just an hour away from Six Flags Discovery Kingdom, I'd never been there before.

An hour in, it was very clear to me why that was.

Chloe pulled me through the park, blowing past stands for funnel cakes and booths sporting games that offered stuffed animal prizes. She eyed the rides around us like a kid in a candy store. She'd tried to get me warmed up with a few meant for small children, which was pretty embarrassing, but it hadn't really worked. Next had been Bumper Cars, which was the highlight so far. The spinning tea cups afterward had made me nauseous, but getting that one over with early on was probably for the best given that I'd been getting hungry.

"Why don't we do one to cool you down, and then we'll ease into the coasters?" she eventually suggested.

"I can't do coasters," I insisted. "I really can't."

"Just one," she pressed. "For me? Please?"

She reached out and squeezed my hand, and I gave in when I realized she was about to go for an over-exaggerated pout. "One."

"Yes! I'll take it! And since you've never been on any before, who knows? You might actually like it."

"I won't," I insisted, but she was already dragging me off again.

Her "cool-down ride" idea was literal. We stepped into line for a ride down a river in an eight-man circular raft behind three guys that looked about our age, and thirty minutes later we were still only three-quarters of the way to the front of the line. Right around then was when one the guys noticed us.

We were sitting side by side on the top of the wooden fence meant to keep us neatly organized in our immobile line. Chloe was swinging her feet back and forth beneath herself and accidentally lost control of her momentum, sending herself backwards with a loud squeal. With my help, she caught herself before she actually fell, but that didn't stop my heart from going haywire in the milliseconds between her fall and our joint save.

"Whoa, you okay?" one of the boys in front of us asked her. He gave his head a sharp shake to get his shaggy brown hair out of his eyes, and I hid a grin. Two seconds had passed and he already couldn't take his eyes off of Chloe.

Chloe, to her credit, played it off like a champ. "Yeah, totally fine. I meant to do that."

He laughed at her joke like it was much funnier than it was, and she smiled back. "Cool. So are you guys from around here?"

"San Francisco," Chloe confirmed. "I'm Chloe. This is my friend Harper."

"I'm Josh. These are my best friends Pete and Hunter. We're here with Pete's parents on vacation."

"How do you like it here so far?"

Josh grinned widely. "It's awesome." He leaned in closer, like he didn't want anyone to overhear, and added, "The girls here in Cali are, like, really hot. It's like you guys are all models or something."

"I know, right?" Chloe agreed. That made Josh and his friends laugh. I turned away and tuned them out, frustrated that she was even humoring them when they were so obviously flirting with her, and Chloe's amused look told me she'd noticed. The line started to move again.

"We're having a barbecue at the condo we rented out tomorrow night," Pete spoke up at some point.

"We're pretty much inviting anyone cool we meet. You should come. And your friend."

"What's your name again?" Hunter asked me before Chloe could reply.

"Harper." I tugged at Chloe's arm and leaned in close to hiss in her ear, "Fine. You win. Let's go to the coaster."

"Guys, it was really nice to meet you, but we actually have to go," Chloe told them abruptly, her hand finding mine as she spoke. "This line's a killer. We're gonna go find some coasters. Have a good vacation!"

She pulled me out of the line and I followed obediently, hurrying after her down the winding path that led back to the entrance. I heard one of the guys shout something to us as we left, but I couldn't make it out. He sounded hopeful.

Chloe was laughing as we reached the bottom, and she only laughed harder when she turned around and saw me scowling at her. "The look on your face!"

"We were *not* going to that barbecue."

"Of course not. But it was to worth it to see you squirm. Relax; they're just boys. C'mon!" She pulled me onward without warning, and I wrinkled my nose with disgust.

"The Bieber one was looking at you like a piece of meat!"

* * *

"Breathe."

The attendant secured the straps meant to keep me from death with a not-very-satisfying series of clicks. Then he moved ahead to the next car. I squeezed Chloe's hand so tightly I was surprised she wasn't in pain.

"You're amazing," she insisted, lips so close to my ear I could feel them brushing against it. I wasn't sure if my lightheadedness could be attributed to that or to my impending doom. "I'll buy you an ice cream cone when we get back to the bottom, alright? Can you at least do chocolate sprinkles?"

"Negative."

"My god."

"I know."

She exhaled slowly, and I swallowed hard as the bar in front of us lowered over our laps. It clicked into place and I tried not to hyperventilate. Beside me, Chloe muttered, "At least I never showed you *Final Destination 3*."

"Wha-?" I started to ask, but the coaster rolled forward and I clamped my mouth shut. Chloe let go of my hand and I looked over at her, wide-eyed.

"You're gonna want to be hands-free," she explained. "It's not a good ride if it doesn't wanna make you throw your hands up and scream. That's what Dad says, anyway."

"That's not comforting at all," I half-whimpered.

"It's just a left turn right now," she told me. "Just take it a little at a time."

The left turn she spoke of took us around a bend,

and for the first time, I saw just exactly what I was dealing with. Chloe'd told me there were no loops or inversions. That was true. She'd failed, however, to mention the ascension into the *clouds* and the drop that'd follow.

"I'm gonna die."

"I'm with you," she reminded me. "You're not going anywhere." As we began our ascension, it occurred to me that it was actually my presence guaranteeing Chloe's safety rather than the other way around.

"What's *Final Destination 3*?" I asked her at last, mostly to take my mind off of our impending drop.

"Trust me, you definitely do *not* wanna know that right now."

"Yes I do."

"Nope."

"Just tell me. If we talk I'll stay distracted."

"It's a horror movie. I'll tell you at the bottom. While you're eating your vanilla cone tragically lacking chocolate sprinkles."

"But I wanna know now."

"Harper-"

"But-"

"Put your hands up," she told me abruptly, and I took my eyes off of her and faced forward as momentum and gravity did their jobs.

I think I blacked out for the first drop. There was a vague memory of my stomach dropping and Chloe screaming happily – because that's apparently a *thing* insane people who like roller coasters can do –

next to me, and then we were at the bottom and zooming up and down and around the wooden track and *everyone* was screaming and cheering except for me. I kept my jaw locked, my teeth gritted, and my hands firmly attached to the bar over my lap for the first half of the ride, and then I felt Chloe's lips far too close to my ear again and there was a giggly tone to her voice as she shouted, "Just let go!"

I shook my head silently, and she put one hand over mine and pulled gently. "Just one!" she insisted, and I relented, sure I looked ridiculous with one arm in the air and my fingers interlocked with Chloe's as she screamed wildly over the next drop. I attempted a small squeal that sounded more like a dying seal than anything else, and then kept my mouth firmly shut for the rest of the ride.

When it finally came to an end and we were freed, my legs were wobbly. Chloe found that hilarious.

I sat on a bench just outside the ride while Chloe went to get ice cream, and by the time she came back, I'd managed to catch my breath. "So what'd you think?" she asked, grinning. "Kinda fun? Just a little?"

"That was an experience," I conceded. "One I'll never have again, but I'm sure when I'm old I'll cherish this memory. Really, *really* old."

"I'll take it." She took a seat next to me and handed me my cone. "We can go do the kiddie rides again."

"No way. You should go find your dad," I

suggested. "I can hang out with your mom while you guys do all the scary stuff."

"You don't have to do that. I'm not gonna leave you alone with my mother just so I can ride some extra rides. I'll do it some other time."

"That's sweet. Thank you." I smiled at her, licked at my cone, and then, mouth full, demanded, "Go find your dad."

"Harper-"

"Chloe, go. Seriously. It won't kill me to get to know your mom. Just be careful."

"You sure?" She looked concerned, but one of her legs was bouncing with excitement. She probably hadn't even noticed.

"Positive. Just tell them to meet us here and we'll switch up the pairs. No big deal."

A smile broke out across her face and she squealed quietly as she threw her arms around me, ice cream cone and all. "You're perfect."

"Remember this moment next time I host a Marilyn Monroe themed movie night, no action movies included," I mumbled and then laughed when she groaned into my neck.

* * *

Mrs. Stephens and I went straight to the kiddie section of the park, where I belonged, and spent a couple of hours embarrassing ourselves by being the only guests in the park over four feet tall on almost everything we rode.

"I never got to take Chloe on these types of rides

when she was a kid," she told me during ride number three. "She and her dad were certainly cut from the same cloth. We couldn't take her to places like this until she met the height requirements for the thrill rides, because otherwise there was no point in going."

"So she's always been like that," I mused. "Total adrenaline junkie."

"She gets it from her father. And his father. Her grandfather passed away about a decade ago, and one of the last things he told her was not to waste a second of life. I swear, that man'll get her killed one day, the way she leaps into things without thinking about them first. I'm surprised my heart's still functioning."

I didn't reply. Our line moved forward, and Hayley shuffled ahead of me. After a moment, I followed, half-hoping for a change in subject.

"So you and Chloe seem to be close. She talks about you quite a lot for someone she's only known a month."

That wasn't exactly the change of subject I'd been hoping for.

Inwardly, I cringed and tried to think of an appropriate response in an appropriate amount of time. But I'd never been anywhere close to in this position before, and the result was a long, awkward silence that Hayley had to break herself.

"Sorry to put you on the spot like that, Harper. You seem like a sweet girl. I'm glad Chloe has a friend. She had trouble back where we used to live."

"Trouble?" I echoed, confused.

"She had some problems with making friends. The kind she could bring home and have sleepovers with. She's always been very blunt and I think a lot of time that doesn't sit well with other kids your age."

"I think I like blunt sometimes," I told her. "Blunt makes everything easier."

She laughed lightly. "Well, at any rate, I'm glad Chloe has you. You have a mother's approval."

I raised a hand to my head to scratch it, but that was only so I could use my palm to hide the eye Hayley could see. I was, very suddenly, a little teary-eyed. "Thanks," I mumbled, hoping I didn't sound choked up and that my voice wasn't shaky. "I haven't heard that one in a while."

Chapter Seven

Chloe rested her head on my shoulder and slept during our ride home. I was exhausted, too, after such a long day. Too exhausted to go camping, especially given that I'd only agreed in the first place after a lot of convincing from Chloe.

When we got home, I nudged her awake while mid-yawn myself, and then admitted, "I just want to go to sleep."

"I know, right? I didn't expect it to be so draining."

"Maybe Dad will let us take a rain check," I suggested. That woke her up pretty quickly. She looked concerned.

"Oh, no, you can't cancel on him. It'll hurt his feelings."

"What if I promise to let him take us next

weekend?" I suggested. "We can spend the whole day at the camp ground instead of just an evening. And we won't just be sitting around yawning the whole time, wishing we were back home in our own beds."

She let out a sigh, like she knew I was just making excuses, but that sigh soon morphed into another yawn and she shrugged her shoulders. "Just try to be nice to him when you tell him."

"I will," I insisted. "I feel bad. But who knows? Maybe they'll want the quality time anyway."

* * *

As it turned out, Dad and Deborah did *not* want the quality time. As Deborah sat quietly beside him on the couch, Dad folded his arms across his chest and said stiffly, "First you didn't want to go. Then you told me you *would* go if Chloe could come along. And now you're telling me that we're supposed to be leaving in ten minutes and *neither* of you want to go?"

"We do! Just... not tonight," I mumbled. "We're tired. We spent all day walking around. We thought we could handle it and we couldn't. I'm sorry. You should go without us."

"We will," was all he said. He wasn't as angry as I thought he'd be, but I had a feeling that had something to do with Deborah being in the room. She wouldn't look me in the eyes as he added, "We'll talk more tomorrow. Go to your room."

I did. And once I was safely inside, I pulled out

my new cell phone and texted Chloe an update. She sent back a frowny face, but I knew she was just as relieved as I was. She'd had even more of an eventful day than I had, thanks to our trade-off and the resulting time she'd spent going on rides with her dad. The two of them were cute together. Kind of the way I wished my dad and I could be, were we both not such homebodies.

It occurred to me, then, as I sat on my bed, that maybe Dad saw some of the same things in Deborah that I saw in Chloe.

* * *

I made plans with Chloe and Robbie the next day, and made sure to leave the house before Dad and Deborah were back. Robbie picked both Chloe and me up and drove us out to my parents' old secret spot by the cliff and the lake-like body of water. We brought bathing suits this time, but I laid out on a towel in the sand with a comic book while Robbie swam around. Chloe stood at the water's edge, clearly antsy, and kept glancing up to the top of the cliff.

"Don't even think about it," I reminded her. "Rocks."

"Yeah, I know," she sighed out, and then waded out into the water. "Come in with us!"

"I'm reading!" I called back.

Once she was deep enough to immerse herself, Chloe flipped herself onto her back and breast-stroked away from me. I felt her judgmental gaze on my face even when I looked away from her.

"What are you reading?" she eventually asked me.

"A comic book Robbie loaned me," I told her.

She laughed. "You guys read comic books?"

Robbie swam toward her and stopped just a few feet from her head, treading water. "It's Batwoman. You might like it."

She scoffed. "I didn't know I was hanging out with *nerds*. Jeez." She flipped around and immersed herself in the water, then swam away without resurfacing. Robbie arched an eyebrow at me.

"She's kidding," I elaborated.

"If you say so."

Chloe came back up for a moment, and I called out to her, "Hey, don't go too far, okay? We don't have life jackets."

"Life jackets and comic books: you're super cool, Harper," she joked and dived down again.

"I can see why you like her," said Robbie.

"She's kidding! Again."

He swam toward me, leaving Chloe behind, until the water was at his knees. He stopped there and sat down on the rocks, relaxing with the water halfway up his stomach. "So, how have you been? Really?" he asked me.

I shrugged my shoulders. "I'm alright. Not great... but alright."

"You can always call me," he reminded me. "I'm just... socially awkward and shit. You know that."

I forced a laugh. "Yeah, I know. I'm glad you

made me leave work early the other day. I needed a break."

"Are you still thinking about quitting?" he asked me.

"Yeah. If I had another way to make money, I definitely would, but as of right now, I don't."

"What about your dad's new girlfriend?" he suggested. "If they get married, your family income just doubled, you know."

I gaped at him. "Oh my god, that's awful. And besides, they definitely aren't getting married any time soon."

"That's probably true." He paused, and then lowered his voice. "So..." Then he turned and looked over his shoulder in a move I instinctively knew was to make sure Chloe wasn't close enough to overhear.

Except Chloe wasn't there at all. The water all around us was calm and flat, and she was just... *gone.*

I tossed Robbie's comic book onto the ground beside me and raced into the water. "CHLOE! CHLOE!"

Robbie was already two steps ahead of me, swimming with everything he had toward the last place we'd seen her. I could only watch helplessly as he pulled ahead of me, arms and legs pumping furiously. I kept my eyes on him as I tried my best to follow, but I felt like my arms and legs had turned to rubber.

"CHLOE!" Robbie screeched ahead of me, but we

both knew by now it was no use. She was underwater.

I scanned the surface desperately, trying to see something, *anything*, but I didn't know what I was looking for. Bubbles? Was that something people just looked for in the movies?

Half of a palm and a few fingers splashed out of the water just a few feet ahead of Robbie, and he surged forward and then dived down. The seconds that passed felt like hours.

Later, the only thing I'd remember was how utterly useless I'd felt from the moment I splashed my way into the water.

Robbie came up with Chloe in his arms. Her hair hid most of her face, but she was already coughing up water. I started to head toward them, but Robbie called out, "Just go put out a towel for her to lay on. I think she's okay; she wasn't under long enough."

I trembled as I did what he'd asked. He carried her all the way out of the water, even as harsh coughs wracked her body, and as he laid her out on the towel, he asked her, "Chloe, you can breathe, right?"

She nodded feebly, but she was trembling even worse than I was. I fell to my knees beside her and brushed her hair out of her face, hands shaking. Another series of coughs expelled more water from her mouth, but the ones after that were dry. As she slowly got her breathing back, I kept a hand on her forehead, my thumb moving back and forth over the center. I didn't realize until she spoke that I'd been covering the number on her forehead with my palm.

"Got my foot stuck on something," she managed to get out, and then let out another series of short coughs. "Tangled, I think. I'm okay."

"We should think about taking her to a hospital to make sure," Robbie told me. "I don't know a lot about what nearly drowning does to someone."

"I'm okay," Chloe repeated. Her voice was hoarse and weak. "I coughed it all up." She closed her eyes and took in a slow breath, and then exhaled just as slowly. When she spoke next, her voice was a little stronger. "Yeah. I'm okay."

Robbie and I exchanged looks, and I saw him relax a little. But his gaze held mine long enough that when it slid to my hand on Chloe's forehead, I knew we were thinking the same thing. As Chloe kept breathing slowly beneath us and her eyes fluttered shut, I stared down at the back of my hand. In that moment, only two thoughts were running through my head. Over and over again, back and forth, until I was sure that when I blinked I could see them in sentence form behind my eyelids.

The first was that Robbie had just prevented Chloe's death. The second was that *I* hadn't been able to do a single thing to help.

I moved my hand, and felt my rib cage cave in and crush my heart. My head dropped and I let out a sob as, at last, the tears I'd been holding back began to flow. And no matter how many times Chloe murmured, "Hey, I'm okay, I'm okay, Harper," I

112

couldn't bring myself to stop. I couldn't even look at her.

16.

* * *

Dad sat with me on the couch for a little while after Robbie took me home. Deborah made me a mug of hot chocolate while he rubbed my back, but none of that helped. I didn't want to be home with them. I just wanted to be with Chloe.

Robbie'd gotten her parents' phone numbers off of her cell phone and called them, and by the time we'd gotten back to Chloe's house, they'd been poised to take Chloe to the hospital themselves. Thankfully, that was just precautionary; she'd been practically back to full health by the time we'd gotten back, other than a couple of coughing fits every now and then. She didn't understand why I was still so upset.

I could tell that once Chloe was with her parents, Robbie wanted a chance to talk to me. Or comfort me. I didn't know. But that wasn't his place, even if he was the only one who could do it properly given the circumstances. Chloe nearly drowning had been a shock to my system, but seeing her number still there, unchanged even after Robbie had saved her, had done the real damage.

It meant that Robbie was right. It meant that Chloe had never been meant to drown today. When her time came, no amount of planning would stop it. *I* couldn't stop it.

Chloe was going to die, and she was going to die soon. And there wasn't a single thing I could do about it.

* * *

"Sooo... predictably, nearly drowning sucks."

"I can't right now, Chloe," I sighed out, phone pressed into my ear as I lay splayed out on my bed. "I'm sorry. Not yet."

"You don't have to apologize. I get it; it's too soon."

"No, I do have to, because joking is how you deal. But I just can't joke about it." I paused as my throat tightened, and tried to push the feeling away. "I just remember looking past Robbie and you were gone and we couldn't find you. And now I can't even see you."

"Hey," she replied, her voice taking on a soothing tone I hadn't ever heard from her before. "Hey, I'm okay now. It was a freak accident and I'm okay. I promised I wasn't going anywhere, remember? My parents are just a little freaked and they don't want to let me out of the house yet. At least they let me see you for a few minutes yesterday...?"

"It wasn't enough," I muttered.

"I know. But I'm just gonna take a few days to cool off, and then I'll be over to go on that camping trip with your dad and his girlfriend. Our double date camping trip."

I forced a laugh and wiped at my eyes. "Okay."

"Will you be okay tonight?"

I nodded, and then remembered she couldn't see me. "Yeah. Robbie's over right now."

"Good. Tell him thanks for the thousandth time for what he did. Even though I was totally just about to save myself, I swear."

"Chloe-"

"Okay, sorry, no jokes. I'll text you all day and call you a hundred times until the weekend comes, alright?"

"Promise?"

"Promise."

The call ended on her end with a soft click, and I put my phone down and looked over at Robbie, who sat at my desk chair with his head in his hands. He shot me a sympathetic look.

"Feel any better?"

I shrugged. "I don't know. How can I feel good about this? I mean... you were right."

"I didn't want to be." He avoided my eyes, picking at something on the back of his hand, and then asked, "So where do we go from here?"

"We?" I echoed.

"If you think I'm letting you go through this alone after what just happened three days ago, you don't know me at all. I carried her out of the water and watched her cough up a lung. She called me a nerd and made fun of my comic books, so I'm in this with you now." He gave me a small smile when I let out a weak laugh.

"I'm glad you're my best friend," I told him.

"Me too." He sat back in the chair and folded his

arms across his chest. "We're strong people, Harper. This won't be fun, but we've been here before with people who were family. We can get through it again. And this time, we can stop being in denial and stop making lists and taking extra precautions that won't change anything. This time we can help someone use the days they have left the way they should be used. In a way that doesn't waste them. And I know that it's morbid, and that it'll be hard, but-"

"But if we were Chloe, we'd want it this way," I finished for him. "I know. I can do it."

"You don't have to do it alone," he reminded me. "In fact, I'm not going to let you do it alone. If..." He paused and seemed to struggle through the next word. I was long past choked-up; I'd given up stopping the tears several minutes ago, on the phone with Chloe. "When," he corrected at last. "When she doesn't make it through the summer, I'll be right there with you helping you deal."

I nodded silently and wiped at my eyes. I could tell he meant every word.

A long silence passed between us, and I sniffled one last time and then told him, "Chloe says thank you for saving her. Again."

"Tell her anytime," he replied, and he sounded so sincere that, for just a moment, he made me forget it was impossible.

* * *

Having Robbie around made everything much

easier that week. It made life in general feel so much more manageable. And during that week, I think I finally started to realize that just spending time in the presence of a single person over and over again didn't necessarily make them a friend.

Robbie'd been a person in my life, and he'd been someone to talk to about our shared experience, but we hadn't ever really clicked just because we *could*. Days spent playing laser tag or reading comic books together had been few and far between and had completely stopped right before I'd met Chloe. I'd forgotten what it was like to have a real friend before her. I'd figured Robbie was it: someone I just went through the motions with. Someone I just spent time with, even if most of the time I didn't enjoy it, and even if it didn't make me feel particularly good.

Chloe made me feel good. And Robbie would never be Chloe, but knowing that he was there for me, and that he was trying to bite his tongue when his more cynical side started to show, and that he actually *cared* about what happened to Chloe, made me think I could eventually be okay when she was gone. Like maybe he could actually be a friend I'd enjoy having around, and like instead of being a fleeting streak of color in my black and white world, Chloe'd started a new era where I could see more than just a few different shades.

I considered giving up old movies.

I considered kissing her the next time I saw her.

* * *

Deborah stayed over the night before we were due to go camping. She, Dad, and I made polite conversation over dinner, and then Dad picked out a movie and went to go pop popcorn, leaving me and Deborah alone in the living room.

"That's a cute shirt," she told me, breaking a long and awkward silence. I glanced down at my oversized pajama shirt and forced a laugh.

"Thanks."

I sat back in the small chair I'd been relegated to and stretched my legs, letting out a yawn. Tomorrow was a big day. It was the first day I'd get to really see Chloe again. The last thing I wanted to do was spend the night beforehand staying up late to watch a movie with my father and his girlfriend, but I felt like I had some ground to make up with my dad. The least I could do was pretend to stay awake through a movie.

"How is your friend? Have you heard from her?" Deborah asked me.

I tilted my head back and forth and listened to my neck creak. Then I cracked a couple of knuckles. Finally, I said, "She's okay now." I paused, and then added, "I didn't know Dad told you about that."

"Well, I'm glad he did."

I snorted and shifted to face her. "Why? You hardly even know Chloe."

"I know she's a good friend of yours."

"Yeah, but you hardly know me, either," I pointed out.

She looked pained, and opened her mouth to say something else, but Dad reentered the room, two bowls of popcorn in his hands. He set one down on my lap and then moved to sit beside Deborah with the other.

"Alright, let's get this thing rolling," he said, and raised the remote to point it at the television. He pressed play, and the movie began.

I drifted off halfway through, somewhere between daydreaming about Chloe and me alone in a tent and remembering what it'd felt like to look out at the water and not see her there.

When my dad shook me awake at the end of the movie, I couldn't remember which had made my heart pound faster.

* * *

Chloe rang our doorbell at nine in the morning the next day, while I was halfway through putting my hair up in my bathroom. I abandoned it immediately to race downstairs and throw open the front door.

She was there, a backpack on and sporting a grin that mirrored my own. When she launched herself forward into my arms, I was mostly ready, and when she threw her arms around me, I hugged her back even tighter. Her lips brushed against my shoulder as she murmured, "I missed you," and for a moment, everything felt right in my world.

Then she pulled away, caught sight of my hair, and literally pointed and laughed at me. I swatted at her arm and tugged at the elastic that'd been holding my hair half-up. With a quick pull, it was released, and down fell my hair in every direction, making Chloe laugh harder.

"I've missed you, too," I deadpanned.

She grabbed my hand and led me upstairs, declaring, "I'm going to help you get ready."

And that was how five minutes later I found myself sitting on a stool in my bathroom with Chloe's face inches from mine and an eyeliner pencil pressed to my eyelid.

"This seems unnecessary. We're going camping," I pointed out.

"Don't complain; I'm doing it for you," was all she said.

I closed my mouth and let her finish. Her face was far too close to mine for me to truly be complaining, and to be honest, I kind of liked the attention.

"God, you're beautiful," she sighed out. "If I wasn't so busy wanting you, I'd *so* want to be you."

"I missed you," I told her again, and then watched her reach for a container of lip balm in my makeup bag. She dipped her index finger inside and then looked directly at me for a moment before her gaze dropped to my lips.

"Open."

I laughed at first, and then what she was asking sank in and I barely managed to choke out a "What?"

"Open. Your mouth," she elaborated. "It's going

to get cold tonight and your lips are going to get dry, and then they'll crack, and then you'll be glad I had the foresight to do this."

"Pfft. Foresight my ass," I muttered, but did as she said. She hid a smug look – although not very well – and then leaned in close and made a big show out of slowly tracing my bottom lip with her finger. I swallowed hard when she was done.

She leaned back and stared at me for a moment, and then arched an eyebrow. "Aren't you gonna rub them together?"

I blinked at her. "Huh? Oh." Reddening, I rubbed my lips together and then leapt from the stool. "Okay, so now-"

"Hey, I wasn't done," she cut in gently. "You can't leave without a mirror check. Duh." She took me by the shoulders and turned me around to face the mirror. I didn't spend more than a second looking at myself. Chloe and I stared at each other in the mirror for a moment, her hands still on my shoulders, and then I took a quick breath and turned around to face her. She instinctively moved away to give me space, but I shook my head quickly and grabbed her side, holding her close. She glanced down at my hand and then at me, and it occurred to me that for all her bravado, she looked just as nervous as I felt.

I opened my mouth to try to speak, realized I had no idea what I was doing or what I wanted to say, and then closed my mouth again. Chloe didn't seem to want to make the first move. I didn't really blame her given how that'd gone for the past month or so.

I fixed my gaze to her lips and watched her lick them. It felt like it took all the strength in my body to move the couple of inches forward that it took for our noses to brush. I saw her close her eyes and so I closed mine, then wondered how I'd kept them open in the first place, as heavy as they felt now. My twenty-pound hand somehow made it from her waist to her cheek, and I stepped in so close I was sure I could hear her heart beating. Or maybe that was my own.

"Girls, are you-? Oh."

Chloe turned her head so sharply her ponytail swung around and whacked me in the side of my cheek. Flushing deeply through a wince, I didn't have to look to see it was Deborah standing in the bathroom doorway. She was even more embarrassed than Chloe and me, judging by the look on her face. She was so red that for a moment I wondered if Dad had even told her that I was a lesbian.

"I'm sorry, Harper, your dad asked me to come check on you, I'll tell him-" she rushed to say, but Chloe cut her off, sounding surprisingly calm.

"It's okay, we'll head down now. We were just, um, finishing up Harper's makeup. For the camping trip." She scratched at the back of her head awkwardly and then shuffled past Deborah without looking back at me. Once she'd gone, Deborah and I stood alone in the most uncomfortable few seconds of my life.

"I'm sorry," she said at last. "I didn't know-"

"That I liked girls," I finished for her.

She smiled feebly, still as thoroughly embarrassed as I was. "No, I knew. I didn't know that you and Chloe were-"

"We're not," I said, stopping her. "So... thanks."

I slipped past her and headed for the stairs, willing my blush to fade before I reached my dad.

When I found him, he was with Chloe in the living room. She was talking to him like everything was fine, but she couldn't quite look me in the eyes.

"Alright, Harper, ready to go? All packed?" he asked me when he caught sight of me.

I nodded. "My bag's by the door."

"Great." He smiled at Deborah, who must've shown up behind me just then, and asked her, "Would you like to lead the way?"

"Lead the way?" I echoed. "Are we taking two cars?"

"Yes," said Dad. "You and Chloe can take your car. That way if the two of you wind up chickening out, you can leave without us."

"I won't chicken out," I insisted, but I mostly just didn't want to ride alone with Chloe. Her facial expression said she felt the same way, and she even chimed in to agree with me.

"Yeah, Mr. Locklear, don't worry. We'll be okay."

Dad seemed skeptical, but after a few-second pause, Chloe's input seemed to win him over.

"Alright, but I don't want to hear any complaints." He headed for the door and I trailed after him, avoiding eye contact with Deborah along the way.

I'd gotten out of being alone in a car with Chloe. Now if only I could get out of being alone in a tent with her all night, because it certainly looked like it was going to be a long one.

* * *

A half-hour drive precluded our arrival at the campground, but I convinced Dad to crank up the music during the drive, so it wasn't bad.

We pulled into the campground and unloaded our stuff from the back of the car. Dad and Deborah carried most of our gear, but my backpack wasn't exactly light, and I wasn't looking forward to carrying it all the way to our campsite.

Deborah led the way down a trail near the parking lot, and Dad brought up the rear, leaving Chloe and I to linger awkwardly in the middle. Eventually, the distance between the two of us and both Deborah and Dad widened, and Chloe decided it was time to acknowledge me.

"So, um... I didn't mean to." She paused like she was hoping I'd say something, but I didn't. Sighing, she continued, "If I did anything, I mean... I was just-"

"Look, I like you," I finally blurted out. Chloe tripped over a root and nearly fell, and I attempted a feeble catch that only made things worse and sent us both sprawling to the ground.

"Whoa!" Dad called out behind us, and I heard

him up his pace. Ahead of us, Deborah stopped walking, but I was too busy trying to push myself up off of a wide-eyed Chloe to see either of them until they were at our sides.

"Sorry, that was my fault," I mumbled.

"I'm okay. We can keep going," Chloe agreed, and shot me a sideways look. The four of us moved as a tight-knit group after that, which was absolutely painful, and I thought wryly that at least the day couldn't get any more awkward.

We found our campsite not long after that and got the tent parts laid flat on the ground. Deborah moved toward me like she wanted to help me out with mine, but I grabbed Dad before she could reach me, so she mercifully went to work on her and Dad's tent with Chloe's help.

They finished first. Dad and I were kind of pathetic. Our tent fell over every which way before Deborah finally felt sorry enough for us to come help. As I watched her, I had to admit that she seemed like a pretty cool woman. If she were a teacher of mine rather than my dad's girlfriend, I knew I'd like her. But as it was, I couldn't help but have trouble warming to her, and this morning certainly hadn't helped.

We spent a few hours by a nearby lake after that. Deborah knew how to fish, which wasn't surprising, but she wanted to try and teach me and Chloe how to do it too. After giving us instructions, she set us up a decent distance from her and Dad, which I knew was her way of giving us time to talk. I didn't appreciate it.

Chloe and I sat in silence for a long time while I half-assed a cast out into the water with an un-baited hook. I didn't like the idea of catching fish. The catching part sounded fun, but I couldn't get past the idea of some poor unsuspecting fish getting a hook in the mouth.

Chloe seemed to put some genuine effort into it, but I got the impression it was out of some combination of her usual "try everything once" philosophy and of her wanting something to focus on other than me, rather than out of a genuine urge to learn how to fish. For that half-hour or so that we spent sitting together without speaking, I jokingly thought about how easier this conversation would've been if one of us were a boy. Boys were used to initiating conversations.

She cleared her throat at last, and I nearly let out a sigh of relief when I realized she was actually going to speak.

"Sooo... this is awkward."

I grimaced. "This whole trip is awkward."

She wrinkled her nose and nodded her agreement. There was a pause. "...Do you think your dad and his girlfriend are going to do it in their tent?"

"Oh my god!" I screeched and started whacking her over and over on her shoulder while she shook with quiet laughter. "Why would you say that? Why would you put that into my head?"

"It broke the ice, didn't it?" she countered,

grinning at me when I finally gave her a reprieve. "It's better than not talking."

"That's not for you to decide. Eww." I shuddered and set my fishing pole down on the ground next to me.

"It'll be okay," she reassured me. "If we hear any shenanigans coming from their tent, we can fight back with some of our own."

"You..." I opened and closed my mouth for a second, horrified, and then finished, "You need to be on some sort of medication."

"Who's worse: the crazy person or the person who *likes* the crazy person?"

"The crazy person who likes the person who's crazy enough to like the crazy person," I muttered, and she looked at me like she wasn't sure whether to laugh or to kiss me.

For a moment, I thought she might do both, but then she arched an eyebrow, murmured, "Touché," and then went right back to fishing.

Chapter Eight

Given that our fishing abilities were pretty abysmal, and given that I didn't even like the taste of fish in the first place, there wasn't much for me to eat come nighttime. Dad built a fire in a pit that came with the campsite, and I ate canned fruit, then roasted some marshmallows and had them with graham crackers. At one point, Chloe offered me part of a Hershey bar, then got a horrified look on her face and quickly withdrew her offer with a sympathetic shake of her head. I hid a grin as I took a bite of my chocolate-less s'more.

Dad told scary campfire stories and I pretended like they actually crept me out, all while Chloe cracked up and Deborah stared at Dad with the same expression I caught Chloe watching me with every now and then. I toyed with the idea of calling a truce with her at one point, but then Chloe took my hand and squeezed and my mind was elsewhere.

At last, we retreated to our tents to change clothes and go to bed. Chloe and I had a simple setup: two sleeping bags, side by side, with our feet by the door to the tent. Our pillows were cold from being exposed to the air while we'd eaten by the fire, but the longer I rested my head on mine, the warmer it became. As Dad and Deborah drifted off to sleep in their tent, the sound around us faded. Soon, we were left with just the crickets and each other, Chloe facing me with droopy eyelids and a light smile on her lips.

"I like the idea of falling asleep next to you," she told me and burrowed deep into her sleeping bag like she was embarrassed, until I couldn't see any part of her face below her eyes.

"Me too," I said simply and reached out to tuck a strand of her hair behind her ear. I hoped she couldn't see my hand trembling. I felt way too nervous for someone with a crush I knew was mutual. My stomach sank when I remembered what made our situation less than perfect, and then I marveled at the fact that I'd so easily forgotten, even for just a few hours.

"We should make sleeping side by side our thing," she told me, her voice muffled by her sleeping bag. "Like, forever."

"I think they call that marriage," I laughed, my voice a whisper.

"I'm okay with that," she mumbled sleepily. Her

eyes fluttered shut, and I brushed my thumb back and forth along her cheek, just watching her.

When she fell asleep, I rolled over, trying my best to do the same.

Except I couldn't. Even with Chloe safe and sound beside me, I couldn't close my eyes without encountering some horrible vision of her dying a terrible death. This past week, I'd been texting Robbie in situations like these, but my dad had confiscated my phone earlier today to prevent me from texting my way through our camping trip.

Eventually, I gave up on sleeping and moved to grab a blanket and a sweater. Then I left the tent.

I walked a few feet away, careful to be quiet, until I found a patch of grass near the fire pit, inside of which a small fire still crackled.

The ground looked soft there, so I laid the blanket out across the grass by firelight. Once I'd finished, I laid down on the blanket, hands behind my head, and let out a slow exhale as I stared up at the stars.

As if I hadn't already dwelled on it enough, I thought about the past week and of the revelation that Chloe's 16 wasn't going to change with a large pit in my stomach. I closed my eyes and took a deep breath. I'd been walked through this breathing exercise before, back when I'd had panic attacks as a kid. In through the nose, out through the mouth. Slow and steady.

My heart rate slowed after a few minutes of this, and at last, I opened my eyes again, feeling calmer but not reassured. We were well into July now, which meant that Chloe's late-August birthday was getting way too close for comfort. Even if I couldn't save her, I had to figure out what I was going to do to *help* her, and quickly. Plus, there was the added matter of deciding what I was going to do about whatever was happening between us. I'd almost kissed her twice today, yet I didn't feel comfortable calling her my girlfriend. Just the thought of taking that step with the knowledge of what was going to happen to her was painful, and now I felt silly for even entertaining the idea today.

I heard her voice before her footsteps, quiet and a little groggy. "You're beneath the stars. I'm sensing an existential crisis."

I sat up and turned around to see Chloe standing just outside of our tent, one hand rubbing at an eye. "I'm sorry. I thought I was quiet enough," I said.

"It's okay. I wasn't ever gonna get a good night's sleep on the ground, anyway. Mind if I join you? I can pretend to find constellations with you."

"I don't know any constellations," I told her, but moved aside to clear a space for her on the blanket. She sat down next to me, knees pulled up to her chest, and smiled.

"What brings you out here, then?"

"Couldn't sleep." I tilted my head back to look skyward again and let out a deep sigh. "I don't think I like it out here."

"Me either," Chloe admitted. "Camping's not my kind of adventure." She paused, and then added,

"What a day, huh? I can tell your dad's happy you finally did this with him, though."

"Yeah. I guess so."

"You should spend more time with him," said Chloe. "He's your family."

"We used to. We'd watch old movies together almost every night back when Mom first died. Just the two of us."

"Ah. So he's the culprit," Chloe joked, leaning over slightly to bump my shoulder with hers.

"No, those movies were my idea," I corrected. "I got really into them right after Mom. Before that it was cartoons and *Buffy the Vampire Slayer*."

"Why?"

"Uh... because I was eleven and Sarah Michelle Gellar plus lesbians is a winning combination?"

She laughed. "No, why the movies?"

"I don't know." I shifted forward and then lay down again, shrugging my shoulders up at Chloe once I was comfortable. "I caught one on TV one day, I guess, and never looked back."

"I think they're boring," she told me honestly, and joined me on her back a moment later.

I forced a laugh. "Yeah, I know."

"Not enough special effects."

"Well, I guess I figured it'd be nice to be taken back to the past. You know how when you read a book or watch a show and you get absorbed into it, and it's like you're in a different world? I like being taken back into the 40s, the 50s..."

"Not in the literal sense, I would imagine," she

deadpanned. "The rampant sexism and homophobia kind of makes it hard for me to romanticize the past like that."

"No, I know. It's not like that." I struggled for the right words. "It's just... I guess the more I absorb myself in the past, the less I have to think about the future, or the now. Things seemed... simpler back then. And it doesn't hurt that some of the movies are actually really good."

"Throwing yourself into the past to avoid the present and future. That sounds healthy." She shot me a sardonic smile.

"Yeah, yeah," I mumbled. "We all have our issues. I just want to be happy. Ignoring things makes me happy. Ignorance is bliss, right?"

"I didn't get the impression that that's what you wanted," she replied idly. "I thought you were more about not being unhappy."

"Is there a difference?"

"Sure. If you want to be happy, it's pretty simple: you do things that make you happy. If you don't want to be unhappy, you're cool with that safe, neutral, boring zone where nothing good *or* bad happens."

"I don't think there's anything wrong with that."

"No, I don't either, if it's what you want. Staying safe in the laser tag corner, right?"

"I can literally feel the sarcasm," I said, turning my head to raise an eyebrow at her. "What's your big goal, then?"

"What, like a life goal?" she asked. I nodded, and

she turned away, crinkling her nose as she thought. Finally, she said, "You first."

"We've already established mine," I reminded her. "To live a boring, uneventful life with as little pain as possible."

"But I don't think *you* think that's what it is." She grinned over at me. "If you could give yourself *one* life goal... like if you were on your deathbed and if you'd accomplished this, you'd be okay with dying... what would it be? Because I don't think it's living a painless life. If that's your number one, that's incredibly sad, and I refuse to believe that your thoughts on your own existence are that morbid. There has to be something you want more than that."

She arched an eyebrow at me, almost challengingly, and I had to work hard not to smile back. "Okay. Do I have to be realistic?"

"Yes. No wishing you'd been able to fly," she murmured. Her teasing look was gone and she seemed genuinely curious now.

I stared back at her, eyebrows furrowed, and thought back to a conversation I'd had with Robbie at least a dozen times now: Whether or not any of our decisions could make a difference in our lives. Whether or not life was all just predetermined and hopeless. Whether or not it was possible to control our own destinies. After Chloe's near-drowning, it seemed more and more likely that that wasn't the case.

I licked my lips before I replied, my voice quiet, "I

think that if I knew, for a fact, that a decision I'd made had changed something... like, *really* changed it... for the better, I think I'd be okay with dying."

Chloe's eyebrows furrowed, her face just inches from mine. "What do you mean?"

"I mean I want to know that this isn't all just meaningless. Like, we aren't born with our whole lives already mapped out by some omniscient force that's already predetermined everything we'll ever say and do and every decision we'll ever make. That idea terrifies me: that we're all just ants under a magnifying glass and someone's poking at us with a stick. Someone who already knows exactly what we'll do and who we'll be and when we'll die. If I could do something that proves to me that isn't the case, I think I'd be alright."

"That's a hard thing to prove. Probably even impossible."

"Yeah. I know."

She shifted slightly, tucking her hands under her cheek, and asked me, "Are you religious?"

"Not really. Are you?"

"I haven't decided."

I forced a laugh. "Doesn't that mean you aren't?"

"No, it means I haven't picked one out. I guess I'm like... spiritual? I think there's probably no heaven or hell. But we can't be the peak of all intelligent life in the universe, because that would be really sad. People are stupid." She let out a sigh, and then smiled at me. "Okay, anyway, I'll go. Mine is simple: I don't want any regrets."

"That sounds like you," I agreed, smiling back at her.

"Your mom told me about your grandfather while we were alone at the park last week."

"She likes you a lot, you know. She told me after we got back. I told her I like you a lot too," she joked.

We stared at each other for a moment, light smiles on our lips, and then I asked, "So what's the plan? How do you die with no regrets?"

"You do lots of scary shit, all totally on impulse," she said very matter-of-factly. I laughed loudly and then hastily covered my mouth, giving my dad and Deborah's tent a furtive look. When I was sure I hadn't woken them, I looked back to Chloe with a roll of my eyes.

"Seriously, though."

"Okay." She paused for a moment, chewing at her bottom lip, and then explained, "I think I turn off a lot of people. I say what I mean, I do what I like. I try not to waste my own time or anyone else's. A lot of people don't like that, but... I kind of see it as doing them a favor. And doing myself a favor. Did you know that one of the biggest regrets dying people have is that they let other people dictate how they lived their lives?"

"I didn't," I replied, even though the question was probably rhetorical.

"Like, they wasted their time doing what other people thought they should do instead of what they wanted to do. So... I figure if I basically say 'screw everyone else' and live for myself, I'm pretty likely to not have regrets. If I want something, I go after it, regardless of what anyone else thinks about me for it."

"Two things," I interrupted. "One: so am I just a conquest?"

"You're a conquest. But you're not *just* a conquest."

"What does that mean?" I asked. I wasn't even sure whether to be offended or not.

"It means you're someone I'm interested in. But being a conquest is only a bad thing if the person chasing is only chasing just to chase, right? I'm chasing you, so you're a conquest. But I'm not chasing you just to chase."

She sighed. "I'm confusing myself. I think I said that correctly, though. Like... I want you. I'm not hiding that. But I'm not wanting you just to want something. As soon as we hung out and got ice cream that first day I knew you were someone I wanted to get to know. And back where I used to live, there were some girls I wanted to get to know and didn't have the courage to talk to, and later I regretted it. This was supposed to be a fresh start, so I decided I wasn't going to do that anymore. Does that make sense?" She looked a little concerned until I nodded.

"Yes."

"I just... I shouldn't have said you were a conquest, I meant that-"

"Chloe, I get it," I laughed, reaching out to touch

her arm. "It's okay. I like that you're like this: that you ramble and tell me everything you're thinking, even if you regret some of the word choices afterward. It's new."

"New in like a refreshing sort of way?" she asked.

"Exactly."

"Okay." She paused, seeming to recall something. "Wasn't there a second thing you wanted to ask?"

"Oh yeah. Um…" I struggled to remember it for a moment. "Oh. I just thought all that stuff you said sounded kind of lonely for someone who thinks *I* close myself off from everyone else."

"Putting what I want over what other people think shouldn't result in my loneliness. That's other people's problems."

"But if a lot of people have the same problem…"

"Look, I don't want those people around anyway. I don't need people in my life who don't want to be around me because I won't do or say what they think I should. I want people who like me for me. I'm okay with not being the most popular person in the world."

I pressed my lips together, sensing she was getting a little heated. "Okay." I hesitated, wondering if my next question was unfair, given what I knew and she didn't. But I couldn't resist asking it. "So what if you died tomorrow?"

Despite what'd happened in the water just a few short days ago, she seemed taken aback by the question. "So what if I did?"

"Would you have regrets? Would you be okay

with it? Would you... I don't know, wish you'd done everything totally differently? Does all this stuff about prioritizing having no regrets apply to you dying as an old lady, or is it applicable now?"

She thought about that for a moment. "I think it's applicable now. I wouldn't be okay with dying now, obviously, and I'd definitely have regrets. I think most people would, because most people plan for a long life."

I studied her, taking in everything I'd learned in the past few minutes. She wanted to die with no regrets. I knew, relatively, when she was supposed to die. If I couldn't stop her death, the best backup plan I could think of was to make sure she accomplished everything she wanted to before she died. Everything within my power, at least. "Like what?"

She raised an eyebrow in question. "Hm?"

"What regrets would you have?"

She laughed at that. "Jeez, we're just laying it all out in the open tonight, huh?"

"I wanna know."

Her smile faded and she stared back at me, like she'd seen something in my expression and was trying to read it. At last, she said, "I'd have to think about it."

"We have all night."

"That's true." She rolled away from me, onto her back, and was silent for a minute or so. Then she began with, "I'd wish I'd have traveled more."

I winced inwardly. There was no way I could

make that one happen.

"I'd regret that I never went skydiving. Or that I didn't push my parents harder for a pet turtle when I was a kid. I'd regret never getting that pink streak in my hair that I've wanted since freshman year and was promised I could get my senior year. I'd regret never experiencing getting drunk and never getting my driver's license... although not at the same time." She laughed and then fell silent, eyes on the stars, and I smiled over at her even as her own faded.

"That's it?"

"I have another," she said, and rolled onto her side again, facing me. "I think I'd have been a little more impatient. I'd have kissed more girls." She paused, and then modified, a hint of a smile on her lips, "Okay, maybe just one more girl. Maybe I would've just locked a bathroom door."

It took a couple of tries to swallow the lump in my throat with her looking at me the way she was. I knew what I wanted, but finding the strength to say the words felt a lot like gathering the courage to jump off of a cliff. "You could kiss me now," I finally murmured.

"I'm not the one scared to love someone," she said. "I can wait."

She shifted closer to me, then, but didn't kiss me. Instead, she nestled into me, her front pressed into my side and her face tucked between my shoulder and neck. Her arm slid over my stomach and her right hand found my left as it rested limply at my side. She interlocked our fingers and squeezed my hand, and my gaze flickered up to the stars overhead.

I was sure, then, with Chloe relaxing beside me and her lips pressed gently against the skin by my collarbone, that if there somehow were a Heaven up there, she'd fit right in.

Chapter Nine

The following Monday, I quit my job. I'd worry about money later; in that moment, the weight off of my shoulders was worth more than any paycheck would ever be. Dad was angry for about a day. The next morning, I was up bright and early with a spring in my step, and he stopped calling me irresponsible right then. He'd tell me later that he'd decided he liked seeing me smile.

Robbie and I went shopping that afternoon, after his shift ended. We bought pink hair dye and hair bleach at the closest general store, and then he grabbed a bottle of vodka while I went to browse in the pet store next door. Eventually, I found a turtle small enough to be easy to take care of but large enough that if Chloe ever officially adopted it,

Baxter wouldn't eat it. I didn't buy it. Yet.

We drove back to my house afterward, the grocery bag in the back seat of Robbie's car.

"Vodka, pink hair dye, and bleach," he said after a long bout of silence. "Do I want to know?"

"I'll tell you sometime," I promised him.

He dropped me off by Chloe's and then left, and I knocked on her door with the bag in my hand. When Kent answered, I subtly tried to hide its contents.

"Hey there, Harper. Let me grab Chloe."

He disappeared inside for a moment, and I bounced up and down on the balls of my feet. When the door opened again, it was Chloe. "Hey!"

"My Dad and Deborah are going out to dinner and staying over at her place tonight," I explained. "So we'd have the whole place to ourselves if you wanted to stay the night."

She grinned. "I'd love to. Just let me check with my parents." She held up one finger and ducked back inside. I heard the sound of muted voices for a few moments, and then she was back. "Let me go grab some clothes."

"I'll meet you at my house!" I called after her, and turned away to jog back toward the road.

"Baxter!" she shouted abruptly, sounding concerned, and a moment later out he came, bounding across the front yard and into the luckily empty road. Chloe came sprinting after him while I cringed at them.

"Sorry, I didn't mean to leave the door open!"

"It's cool; I'll see you in a few!" she called back. I kept walking once I was sure she'd caught her puppy, laughing quietly to myself.

My house was empty when I got home, as expected. I set the bag down on the dining room table and emptied it, then surveyed the contents: the bottle of vodka, which was way too large for just the two of us to get anywhere close to finishing alone, hair bleach, and the temporary dye. I made a mental note to find a good hiding place for the bottle tomorrow morning.

When Chloe showed up with a bag of clothes in her arms, I grabbed the bottle with one hand and the dye with the other, then presented her with both. "Ta-da!"

It took her a second to register what exactly she was looking at, but when she had, she burst into laughter. "Oh my God. You're such a cheeseball. That's pink hair dye!"

"It's totally temporary," I assured her. "It says it'll be out within a week."

"Oh my god." She shifted her gaze to the bottle of vodka. "Is that vodka?"

"Robbie helped me."

She took the bottle from me and eyed it curiously. Then she arched an eyebrow at me. "So the two of us are going to get drunk alone in your bedroom together? That's a terrible idea. Let's do it, c'mon."

She ran for the stairs and took them two at a time, and I grabbed the bleach, a two-liter soda out of the fridge, and two glasses from the kitchen cabinet before I followed her up.

She was waiting in my room, digging through the clothes she'd brought, and as I walked inside, she turned away from me and took her shirt off without any warning, then unhooked her bra. I blinked a couple of times and then averted my gaze, embarrassed, as I put the items in my hands onto my bed.

"We should do the dye first before the vodka, probably," she joked as she pulled on a new shirt. "Otherwise I'm gonna end up looking like Barbie threw up on my hair."

I walked to my own dresser when I heard her changing her pants, and shyly followed her lead. "Okay."

"You know, I didn't tell you yesterday how awesome I think it is that you quit your job," she told me when we were both in pajamas. "Do you feel better?" I nodded. "I thought you would. You're always so wound up. Anything that gets rid of some tension and helps you loosen up at this point is good for you." She glanced toward the bottle of vodka lying on my bed. "Well, in moderation. Come here." She beckoned to me with one finger, and I felt strangely akin to an ant under a magnifying glass as I came closer.

I stopped with a foot of space between us, and she stepped in closer and reached out to gather my hair in her hands. She left a shorter strand free in the front and tied the rest of my hair off, then eyed me appraisingly for a moment before she tugged lightly on the one free strand of hair. "I want this one dyed on me."

"It's right in front," I pointed out.

"I'll find one that'll be under the rest of my hair once we let it down," she said, and then untied my hair.

"Do you need my help?" I asked her. "I've actually never done this."

"I just need you to tell me if it looks okay, and to grab me tin foil. The rest I can handle," she explained.

Half an hour later, I found myself sitting in the bathroom with Chloe, who had a strand of her hair wrapped up in tin foil.

"Tell me your theories on alien life while wait," I suggested, and she rolled her eyes at me, grinning.

"You're such an ass. Except for when you're really sweet." She paused. "Just so you know, you don't have to buy me a turtle."

I frowned and reached for my phone, which I'd left on the bathroom counter. I scrolled through my pictures until I'd found my most recent one, and then turned the phone around to show her. "Her name is Shelley."

Her mouth dropped open and she covered it with her hand to smother a tiny squeal. "She's so cute! You didn't!"

"I just browsed. Just in case," I admitted.

"Harper, you seriously don't have to do all of this," she told me. "I mean, to be totally honest, if

I'd had any idea you were thinking about something like this I would've just left all of the other things out and told you to kiss me." She let out a sigh as she watched me, and I looked away, shrugging.

"Well, that one's happening, too." I paused. "After the alcohol consumption."

That broke the tension, thankfully, and she laughed and shook her head emphatically. "No! I'll kill you if you come anywhere near me."

"You say that now, but we'll see how you feel in an hour," I said, but I didn't really mean it.

* * *

An hour later, Chloe was sprawled out on my bed, an empty glass in her hand and a pink streak of hair buried under several strands of blonde. Her cheeks were flushed and she stared at me, giggling as I cringed at the taste of too much vodka mixed with too little soda.

"Okay," I decided. "You're cut off. So am I." I set my glass aside with some difficulty.

"You're, like, blurry right now," she told me through a laugh. "Woo, three Harpers!"

I snickered and keeled over, my forehead pressed into my mattress less than a foot from Chloe's stomach. "Stop."

"Being drunk is fun. I get why everyone does this." She let out a long sigh. "God, I just wanna make out with you."

I snickered again, then winced when it made my stomach hurt. My voice muffled from the comforter,

I told her, "That's because you're drunk."

"So are you!"

"Not like you," I argued. "I'm responsible."

She laughed really hard at that, and I idly worried for her own stomach. "You got your older friend to illegally buy us alcohol!" She sat up with some difficulty and then shuffled toward me. I felt both of her hands on my cheeks, urging me to sit up. "Harper," she said, sounding serious now, "Come up, I wanna tell you something."

I struggled to raise my head. It felt like it weighed a ton. With Chloe's help, I finally sat up, my legs crossed in front of me while she mirrored my position. She leaned forward and our foreheads crashed together. "Ow!" I complained.

"Sorry. Hey." Her voice was really quiet and her eyes were closed. "So. My stomach doesn't feel great. Either I'm nervous or I'm gonna throw up."

I leaned away from her abruptly, wide-eyed. "Don't throw up on me."

"No, wait." She extended an arm, palm out, and took a few breaths. "No, I'm good. It's just nerves. I wanna say this. Just listen, okay? Are you listening?"

I nodded, then thought better of it when I had trouble focusing on Chloe again. "Listening."

"I, like, am really into you," she told me. I nodded along, processing her words more slowly than usual. "Like, not even just in a kissing and sex kind of way... I mean, totally that way, but sometimes it's like... if I could just, like, press up super close to you and just kind of merge and be this hybrid person I still don't think I'd be as close as I wanna be. And sometimes, like camping day, you'll admit you feel the same way, but I hate how things can never just be easy. We met and we got along great and you like girls and I was like, this is gonna go so well, this is everything I wanted, and you really are. I just wanna be happy and I don't want you to be unhappy, so if I make you happy then why can't we just be happy, you know?"

I blinked at her, and then shook my head. "No, I don't think I got that."

She groaned and fell back on the bed, arms sprawled out at her sides, and whined, "Just kiss meeeee..."

I let out a long sigh and rubbed at one eye, willing the room to stop spinning. "Chloe, you're gonna die," I told her, and then abruptly shut my mouth and stared at her, wide-eyed.

She sat up with a heavy exhale. "Harper, we're *all* gonna die."

"But-"

"You can't be afraid to lose everyone because then you'll have no one, okay?" She reached out and squeezed my hand. "And if you have no one, then, like, you've lost everyone anyway." She pressed her lips together and furrowed her eyebrows. "You know, life kinda sucks, doesn't it? I think I see your point."

"See?" I insisted, poking her. "See!?"

"Well, it's lose-lose in that we're gonna die

anyway, but that's where my idea comes in, see? You make the most of it while you're here. And *you-*" She prodded me in the shoulder, "-don't make the most of it. You're gonna regret that. Like, that's gonna be your regret on your deathbed. I'm gonna wish I'd traveled more, and you're gonna wish you had enjoyed yourself more." She nodded matter-of-factly, as though she'd said the wisest thing anyone ever could, and then let herself drop back onto her back again.

I sighed and crawled up the bed to lie down next to her, and then absentmindedly found her hand with mine before we both drifted off to sleep.

* * *

I woke to a knock on my door and my dad's voice. "Harper?"

"Shit!" I hissed, and raised a hand to my head as the throbbing set in. Chloe was still asleep, drooling rather unflatteringly on the pillow next to mine. I scrambled to hide the vodka and glasses under my bed and then shook Chloe a couple of times before I hurried over to open my door. "Hey, Dad!" I said a little too brightly, but he was too busy looking past me at my bed to notice.

"Oh, Chloe stayed over?" he asked as she sat up and smacked her lips. She hid a pained look and shot him a sleepy smile, and he waved lamely at her. "Guess I'll make a couple more pancakes," he said, and then added, more quietly, "Next time, you need my permission."

"Sorry," I mumbled, and closed the door behind him as soon as he was gone. I turned away and rested my back against it, watching Chloe, and heaved a sigh of relief.

"Holy crap," she said, and raised both hands to rub at her temples. "My head. Never again."

As much as my own head hurt, I couldn't help but smile at her. "You made so much sense last night, Oh Wise One."

"Shut up; I was smarter than you!" she shot back, and chucked her spit-stained pillow at me as I laughed at her.

* * *

"So how was your date last night, Mr. Locklear?" Chloe asked him over breakfast. I shot her a look but she didn't take her eyes off of him.

To my surprise, Dad smiled at her, and then said, "It went well. Thank you for asking."

"Suck up," I mumbled to her, and nudged her foot with mine under the table. She caught my leg with hers and then yanked, nearly displacing me from my chair. Dad arched an eyebrow at the both of us as I replied to her grin with a glare.

"So do you have any plans for today?" he asked us. To me, he added, "Do you plan on finding a new job?"

"Yes," I told him. "As soon as I see one I think I'll enjoy, I'll apply."

"I think I'd like to go back to that spot by the cliff today," Chloe spoke up abruptly. Dad and I had the same reaction.

"You mean the spot by the *water*?" I corrected.

"I'm not so sure that's a good idea," said Dad. "Your parents wouldn't want you there."

"It was a freak accident," Chloe insisted. "I'm okay. I won't go as far out this time." She turned to me and gave me a small smile. "I just thought that after last night I owed you. I want to plan something for the two of us."

I colored abruptly and glanced to Dad, who was watching us with raised eyebrows. Chloe suddenly seemed to realize how badly her words had sounded, and turned red herself.

"It's not how it sounds," I told my dad quickly. "I helped her dye her hair."

"Oh, yeah. Proof!" Chloe perked up and pulled her hair back to reveal the streak underneath. "I've always wanted it done. My parents never let me."

"So you came here and did it while I was out," Dad confirmed, although he looked a little amused. "Now you're definitely not going back to the water without asking your parents first."

"I'll ask," Chloe agreed. She turned to me. "Get a bathing suit on and come over in an hour?"

I shifted uncomfortably. I didn't really want to go anywhere near the cliff or the water after what'd happened last time, but I'd also decided to make a point of letting Chloe enjoy the time she had left. Sighing, I nodded. "Just be careful?"

"I will. Promise." She looked at Dad as she moved to stand. "Thanks for breakfast, Mr. Locklear."

"You can call me Peter, and you're welcome anytime."

"Thanks. And, um, my parents love Harper, so she's welcome anytime, too."

"Good to know."

There was an awkward pause, and I realized Chloe was waiting for me to walk her out. I stood up hastily and headed for the front door, letting her fall into step beside me.

"So do you think you'll regret the pink strand?" I asked her, mostly to make conversation.

She shook her head and smiled. "Never."

We reached the door and she faced me, one hand on the doorknob. She seemed to hesitate for a moment, and then told me, "Harper, I'm really glad I met you."

I nodded, hiding a grin. "I know."

She pressed her lips together in mock-offense. "Say it back."

I knew she was only kidding, and that I didn't have to say it. I also knew that a month ago, I couldn't have said it back. Not with confidence, anyway.

Things were different now. "Chloe Stephens, I am *so* glad I met you."

She bit at her bottom lip for a moment, and then took a deep breath before she spoke again. "So this day by the water that my parents are definitely going to let us have because I'm going to beg them to say yes? I'm gonna call it a date. Okay?"

I blinked a couple of times, and then swallowed

hard and nodded. "Okay."

"Good." She offered me a small smile, reaching out with her free hand to gently squeeze mine. "Your move," she told me, and then slipped out quietly through the front door.

* * *

I got a confirmation text from her fifteen minutes later, and spent the next half hour panicking in my bathroom. One minute I was sure I could take things further with Chloe, and the next I worried about the repercussions of doing so. Robbie's words bounced around in my head: *"If you hook up with her and she dies, you'll be miserable. With that said... If you* don't *hook up with her and she dies, you'll be miserable* and *you'll regret it."*

But if I kissed Chloe, it'd mean more to me than just hooking up with some cute girl. I was beginning to wonder how I could ever live my life happily after losing her. She'd become my best friend.

I put my hair up so that if I decided to get into the water I could still keep it dry. Then I changed into my favorite bikini. When I was done, I tried to ignore the anxious feeling in my chest, and closed my eyes as I rested my hand on my stomach. I remembered the last night with mom; the nausea I'd felt before she'd gone out. I couldn't tell if I was feeling that now, or if this was just regular butterflies.

I made sure to talk to Chloe's parents before we left. They didn't feel very comfortable with where we were going, especially so soon after Chloe's near-drowning, but I think that they, like me, had trouble saying no to her more often than not. And she seemed so excited to go out; she was practically bouncing up and down with anticipation and had packed an entire backpack full of stuff to take with us.

Once we were on our way in my car, she caught sight of the book I'd left on the center console and scoffed. "You are so not reading this whole time. You have to get in the water."

"Not past my waist," I decided.

"Chest?" she bargained. I shook my head. "Okay, what about mid-stomach?"

"Maybe."

"Hey, don't be nervous. We're just hanging out. Nothing bad is gonna happen."

I changed the subject, uncomfortable. "Do you think we've should've brought Baxter? He's been cooped up a lot lately."

"Oh, I didn't even think of that! We should've!" She frowned. "Well, we'll take him next time. He definitely needs to get out of the house more. I've been meaning to keep him active, but, um..." She shrugged her shoulders and finished, "Well, I've been spending a lot of time with you."

Words failed me, and I turned the radio on to avoid an awkward silence. Chloe stretched beside me and then idly turned to look out of her window, her fingernails tapping against the door as she rested her arm on top of it.

We reached the spot by the water all too soon, and Chloe set down her backpack and unzipped it. Out came two blankets, sandwiches, apples, and a pair of sunglasses. She slipped the last over her eyes and grinned at the look on my face.

"You came prepared," I marveled. "Are we having a picnic?"

"Not officially. Too cliché. But you're welcome to a sandwich and an apple." She tossed them to what was then deemed my blanket, and then promptly stretched out across her own, letting out a satisfied sigh. That only lasted a second, as she popped up into a sitting position abruptly and reached for the backpack again. "Oh, right. Forgot sunscreen. I put it in the front pocket. I fry like a lobster." She squirted out a handful and then offered me the bottle.

I shook my head, turning it down. "I'm okay. I don't burn easily."

"Lucky," she sighed out. I sat down on my blanket, which she'd placed directly next to hers, and watched her rub the sunscreen onto her arms, legs, shoulders, and stomach before she laid back down again and grinned over at me. "Try not to stare."

I colored. "I wasn't."

She just laughed and looked skyward again. "So if you want to read while we're here, now's the time. Once I get hot, I'm getting into the water, and you're coming with me."

I shook my head again, but reached for my book

nonetheless. "Sure."

"I'm serious. It'll be okay."

"You're too adventurous," I told her. "I bet half the reason you want to get back in is just for the thrill of it. Normal people like to avoid places they've nearly died at."

"I think of it more as conquering my fears," she said. "Proving to myself there's nothing to be afraid of. It was a freak accident, and when it doesn't happen again, I'll have no reason to be afraid. And neither will you."

"Unless it *does* happen again," I pointed out.

She let out a groan. "Ugh! How many times do I have to tell you that I'm not going anywhere?" She reached over to slap at my arm, teasing, and then went back to tanning. I watched her for a long moment before I cracked open my book to find where I'd last stopped reading.

Even after a few minutes of peaceful silence, I still couldn't manage to shake the uncomfortable feeling that had been building in my stomach all morning. I set my book aside and asked Chloe, "You've never been in love before, right?"

She lifted her sunglasses to look back at me, curious. "Why?" she asked.

"Just wondering."

There was a long pause. "You haven't," she observed. "What makes you think I might have?"

"Because you know what you're doing," I said.

She laughed at that. "Well, I'm glad it seems that way, but no. Never fallen in love, never had my heart broken. All of this is new to me." She paused, blushed, and then amended, "Just to have serious feelings in the first place, I mean. Especially without ever going on a date."

"Isn't this a date?" I joked. She rolled her eyes at me.

"Not unless you eat your sandwich."

I grinned and reached for the baggie that housed my sandwich, then withdrew it and took a bite. As I chewed, I put it back into the bag, sealed it, and then laid back down, facing Chloe again. She studied me as we laid on our sides, and then asked, "Do you want to get into the water?"

I shook my head and responded truthfully. "Not really."

"Well... are you hungry?" she asked. I shook my head again. "In the mood to tan? Or read?" Another head-shake. She laughed lightly. "Then what are we doing?"

I chewed on my lip and willed myself to stay out of my own head before I could even be sucked in by my thoughts in the first place. My head had failed me thus far. It was time to ignore it, and if I waited all day by the water with Chloe, I knew I wouldn't be able to.

Chloe saw my gaze flicker to her lips, and something changed in the way she looked at me. Her lips parted, and I watched her glance down to mine. My heart began to beat heavily in my chest, pressed up against my ribcage. I looked into Chloe's eyes, and then closed my own and moved in closer before I could overthink it.

The kiss wasn't what I'd expected it to be. I'd never really kissed a girl before, or at least not in the way Chloe and I kissed then, and I'd expected pounding hearts and pure passion and roaming hands, like how it always was in modern movies. It wasn't like that. It was, to describe it in a word, tender.

She reached out to cup my cheek with one hand, and we kissed slowly, gently, until I felt the warmth of her body pressing into mine. She shifted, half-leaning over top of me, and we broke apart as I pulled away to lay flat on my back. I stared up at her and held my breath. Her blue eyes were a darker shade as she leaned down to kiss me again.

My stomach churned in that uncomfortable way it had earlier, and I realized it had nothing to do with worrying about her and entirely to do with being a nervous girl on her first date. The realization made me kiss her back harder, and when her hand slid down my bare stomach and settled against my hip I thought I'd die. But then she pulled away again, held her face an inch from mine, and brushed her nose against my own. My eyes fluttered open and I saw her smiling.

"You okay?" she asked me, a certain giddy edge to her tone that made it hard to hold back a smile of my own. I nodded simply and kissed her again. She planted her hands on either side of my head and shifted onto me, and some gracious part of my brain compartmentalized every single one of my reservations and stored it somewhere I wouldn't access until long after we'd parted. For a moment, I forgot about the heartache that came with loving Chloe, and when it finally did begin to come creeping back into the recesses of my mind later that night, when I was alone in my bed, I ignored it.

Some things were worth aching for.

Chapter Ten

My dad took the news well.

I told him over breakfast the next morning, and he arched an eyebrow and replied with, "Oh, really? I was waiting for an update on that. Nice." He offered me a closed fist to bump, and I rolled my eyes at him.

"I don't need Cool Dad; I need Normal Dad. He gives better advice."

He moved his hand away immediately at that. "You need advice? What's going on?" He paused, looking concerned for a moment, and then he sank down in his chair slightly, cringing. "You're not...?" he began, and then sucked in a breath, "sexually acti-?"

"Oh my god, Dad, no," I interrupted swiftly, my face reddening. "And even if I was, I would not want that kind of advice. *Never* that kind of advice."

"Mhmm." He refused to look at me, instead focusing intently on his breakfast. "So, this advice, then."

"You have a girlfriend," I reminded him somewhat awkwardly. "How do you... do things? Like, how do you interact? Is it the same as before you were dating? How do you make that transition beyond turning into a stupid giggly idiot? How do you... be?"

"How do I be. Hmm." He paused to watch me press my palm to my forehead. "Uh, well, I'm not sure I can answer that. You do what feels natural. You also no longer have sleepovers with the door closed or when Dad isn't home for the night."

"I shouldn't have said anything," I decided.

"Probably not," he agreed. "But I'm glad you felt like you wanted to tell me. Even if it was a lapse in judgment." He paused again. "So that camping trip. I went on a double-date with my own daughter."

"That was *not* a double-date," I protested, cheeks aflame.

"You liked her."

"It still doesn't count."

"If she liked you, too, maybe it should." He shot me a curious look. "So... when do I meet her parents?"

* * *

"What is this recipe? My god, it's delicious!"

I slid down in my seat slightly, embarrassed, as I

watched my dad take a large bite of the meatloaf Chloe's mom had made. Chloe, in the seat next to me, bumped my foot with hers. I heard her chuckle quietly.

Hayley grinned at my dad, pleased. "I'll be sure to write it down for you after dinner."

"Please do. Harper likes to mock my cooking, but if I master this, she'll have no reason to complain." He shot me a wink and I rolled my eyes at him.

Dad was a total dork throughout the dinner he'd forced me to set up, of course, but he got along well with Chloe's parents. After dinner, they moved to the living room with glasses of wine, and Chloe and I managed to escape up to her bedroom for a few minutes, where she pressed me up against her door, eyes hooded, tangled her fingers in my hair, and took my breath away.

"We've got to stop meeting like this," I breathed out between kisses, and that made her giggle against my lips, stilling our kissing for a second.

"Shut up, nerd," she demanded, and reached down to hook her fingers through the loops of my jeans so she could gently tug me closer. I'd been laughing, but that stopped very quickly when I felt her hips press into mine. I could hardly think in that moment, but if I *had* been able to think, I'd have wondered how on earth I'd held out on dating her for so long. We'd only been together for a week now and things were already moving so quickly.

She stopped kissing me and started kissing my neck, and I squeezed my eyes shut and moved my hands to her hips, then slid them upward until I could feel skin instead of denim. She did something with her mouth and I dug my nails in.

Chloe made a strange sound against my neck and pulled away abruptly to look at me. "Whoa," she mumbled, her gaze very blatantly on my lips. She inhaled sharply and then declared, "You should spend the night."

I nodded, swallowing hard. "I can do that. If Dad says so."

She nodded back and then abruptly pressed me to the door again, one hand on my cheek and the other on my side. We kissed again, slower this time. I expected our parents to come looking for us at any moment now.

I pulled away first and rested my forehead against Chloe's as we just breathed together for a moment. As my head cleared, I realized, "There's no way my dad will let me spend the night."

Chloe was silent for a moment, and I imagined she was trying to make herself think clearly, too. "Yes," she said at last. "That's not happening. That sucks."

"Yeah. Yeah, it does."

"That's okay. We're teenagers. We're experts at finding a way," she decided, and I moved to press my forehead into her shoulder, muffling a somewhat pained laugh. "Like your car," she added nonchalantly, as though that wasn't one of two three-word phrases that could instantaneously make my face turn red and my heart beat out of my chest.

I wasn't sure I was ready for the other yet, but I was certainly ready for this one.

* * *

"Well, well. You're glowing." Robbie smirked at me as I slid into the passenger's seat of his car. He'd just gotten off work, and we'd planned to go out for ice cream afterward.

"In like a sickly way?" I asked, and he shot me a knowing look.

"No. Do you feel sick?"

"This is the first day since we got together that I won't have seen her," I told him. "I guess I'm paranoid. I shouldn't have waited, and now that we're happy, I feel like it has to end any second. We aren't allowed to be happy."

"You and Chloe? Why not, for just a little while?"

"No, me and you," I corrected. "Not knowing what we know about every single person we look at. Our little 'gift' alone gives me reason to believe something out there in the universe wanted us to suffer. So I have a hard time believing Chloe and I can- that we have a whole month of time, let alone even another week."

"So make the most of it. Isn't that what you've been trying to do? Isn't that the reason you let things get this far?"

"And how awful does that sound? I don't want to rush our relationship just because she might not be around later. I mean, I *do* want to rush it, but I feel bad about wanting to, and I don't even know if I'm even basing my feelings on a rushed timeline or if I'd want what I want regardless of how much time Chloe had left. And I don't want anything we do to be tainted by that uncertainty... if that makes sense?"

"If Chloe knew what you knew, wouldn't she want the same thing?" he asked. "Wouldn't she want to rush?"

"I think she wants to rush *now*," I laughed out. "But that's kind of just who she is."

"So do what feels right." Robbie shrugged his shoulders as we turned into the parking lot of the very same theater I'd taken Chloe all those weeks ago to get ice cream. I smiled vaguely at the memory.

"Thanks, sensei," I told Robbie, and he laughed at me.

"Shut up."

* * *

Chloe and I took Baxter to the local dog park the following day. We sat near the other owners at a picnic table as we watched Baxter speed around the circular enclosure, Chloe's fingers gently intertwined with mine. She leaned her head on my shoulder and I didn't feel self-conscious. Not in San Francisco.

"God, I love it here," she murmured to me, evidently on the same wavelength. "I could live here forever." She paused to watch Baxter bowl over a

166

dog half his size, and chuckled lightly. He'd grown a lot even in the short time since I'd first met Chloe.

"Do you want kids?" she asked me suddenly, and I tensed instinctively before I could stop myself. She raised her head and shot me a soft smile. "I just meant generally, not necessarily with me. Relax; I'm not crazy. I'm just curious."

"I've never really thought about it," I admitted. "I don't think so."

"You don't like kids?"

I just shrugged. Truthfully, I didn't want to chance having a child with a low number. I couldn't go through this a third time.

"I don't feel the need to have kids," Chloe told me, and went back to resting her head on my shoulder. "So that works out."

I let out a laugh despite myself. "I thought we weren't necessarily talking about me and you."

"A compatibility test can't hurt every now and then," said Chloe, grinning. "Besides, I was neutral, so this was a safe question. I just wanted to get to know you. Start planning our future out early, you know?"

She was joking, I knew, but I had to work hard to hide my sadness. "I'd marry you, if we were together for long enough," I told her at last, long after she'd fallen silent again. "I want you to know that."

Chloe raised her head to look at me, a small smile on her lips, and then cupped my cheek in her hand and kissed me softly. "Me too," she murmured against my lips, and my heart only sank further.

With Dad's permission, Chloe was allowed to join me in my room that evening, as long as we kept the door open. I turned on a movie, cut the lights, and we kissed our way through at least the first quarter, until onscreen machine gun fire distracted us long enough to cool us off. I cuddled up next to Chloe, an arm on her stomach, and rested my hand against her heart, counting the beats until I fell asleep.

She was gone when I woke up the next morning. I went downstairs to have breakfast with my dad, who told me, "Deborah and I are going out to a movie tonight. You're welcome to come along if you'd like. You could bring Chloe."

I considered accepting, but then a better idea occurred to me, and I shook my head. "That's okay. I'll stay in. I need a chill night."

"Chill night, huh?" he arched an eyebrow at me. "Alright, well, let me know if you change your mind."

"I will." I forced a smile as he moved to clear his plate off of the table. When I finished, myself, I went back upstairs and immediately texted Chloe: *"No dad at home tonight."*

I didn't get a response immediately, so I took a shower while I waited, then examined myself in the mirror, self-conscious. My stomach was flat enough even if it could use some work; I'd worn a bikini in front of Chloe before and caught her staring. My breasts were around the same size as hers, so there was nothing to be self-conscious about there.

I turned around, looked down, and wrinkled my nose, reminding myself to buy those special shoes that supposedly made butts look better. I'd caught Chloe wearing a pair on a couple of occasions now.

I inhaled sharply at the reminder, and decided I just wouldn't let her see my butt. And I'd take another shower that night, right before she came over. Just in case.

"I am so not ready for this," I mumbled aloud to my reflection. "Get it together. She hasn't done this before, either." I paused. Had she? She'd never said she *hadn't*, but I'd assumed it'd come up at some point if she'd had. What if she had tons of experience and I had none? What if she'd just kept it quiet so that I didn't feel embarrassed?

My phone buzzed in my bedroom and I jumped, then closed my eyes and let out a sigh as my heartrate came back down. After a brief pause, I went to go check Chloe's text.

"Should I come over?"

I hesitated, and not for the reasons I'd talked to Robbie about. I was surprised at myself, because when it came right down to it, my biggest reservations stemmed from my own insecurities about my body and lack of experience. Which were things entirely normal teenagers worried about.

That didn't exactly make me feel any better, however.

"If you want," I sent back. This time I got a text back immediately.

"Do you?"

I stared at the phone for a few seconds. I imagined Chloe waiting with her phone on the other end. I wondered if she was anywhere near as nervous about this as I was. *"I think so,"* I started to type out, but then deleted it and sent instead: *"Yes."*

Her response was instantaneous. *"What time?"*

* * *

I went on a run that day for much longer than I should've, and wound up with achy legs by the time I got back home in the afternoon. It felt silly, but I couldn't help but spend the day nitpicking at every little thing I wanted to fix about myself. I plucked hairs, I moisturized, and I showered two more times instead of just once: another time after my run, and again about an hour before Chloe was due to show up. I wanted everything to go perfectly.

Dad and Deborah left just after nine o'clock, right on schedule, and I made myself not dress up or put a ton of makeup on. Chloe was too confident to do that, and I felt like I'd look lame if I did it and she didn't.

When my doorbell rang ten minutes later than expected, I was surprised to see Chloe breathing hard and looking a little disheveled. She grinned at the sight of me and caught her breath enough to explain, "Your dad told my parents he'd be out for the night, so they wouldn't let me come over. Had to sneak out."

"Oh my God," I marveled, moving aside to let her past me. "Are you gonna get into trouble?"

"Not if they don't know I'm gone," she told me. "Besides, I don't actually care if they figure it out in the morning." She smiled. "I just care that we get to have some time alone before they figure it out."

I nodded, feeling more than a little out of my element, but Chloe just laughed at my expression and took me by the hand, leading me upstairs to my bathroom. "Give me like two seconds to stop looking like a troll?" she requested, and when I nodded, she closed the bathroom door behind herself. I stood, blinking at the door, as I heard the sink begin to run. Then I realized I was being awkward and stepped away to head to my room.

I hadn't really altered it in any way, which I hoped was the right decision. It felt cheesy to light candles or put on music.

I hesitated for a moment, glancing back toward the bathroom door, and then crossed to my bed, sitting on it with my hands in my lap. The sink in the bathroom stopped running, and a few seconds later, Chloe emerged and crossed the hall into my bedroom, pausing in my doorway.

We stared at each other for a moment, and Chloe visibly took in a deep breath, then shook her head and let out a soft laugh. "So I guess we just do this?"

"You have more experience," I countered immediately. "I thought maybe you'd... I don't know. Lead?"

She raised both eyebrows. "I have to-? Oh. Okay. Yeah. Totally. Well, I think once we're making out and everything it should be pretty easy from there."

"Exactly. Totally easy," I joked back, and she smiled, leaning against the doorframe with her eyes on me.

"It felt easy the last couple of times, anyway. Last night and at my house. Would've been easy to go from there." She paused. "This probably works better when it isn't planned, huh?"

I nodded emphatically. "Yes."

"So... maybe we shouldn't plan it? Sure, your dad isn't here, and this might be like the only time we get a chance to do this anytime soon, but we don't have to."

"Right."

"I mean, we'll probably *want* to, but if something feels wrong, we can always wait."

"Ri-... uh." I paused, thinking that one through for a moment. "No," I said instead, eyebrows furrowed.

Chloe looked caught between surprise and uncertainty. "No?"

I shook my head, mentally thanking Robbie for knocking some sense into me yesterday. Chloe wasn't going to be around forever. I wasn't about to stop this because of some slight jitters. "Mm-mm." I stood abruptly before I could lose my nerve, took Chloe by the hand, and tugged her toward my bed. Then I crawled onto it, turned myself over, and sat down, cross-legged, as Chloe stood at the foot of it, watching me.

"So you *don't* want to wait?" she clarified. "Are

you sure?"

"You were the one who said you never wanted to have any regrets," I pointed out. "We don't know what'll happen tomorrow. I don't want to wait."

"That's... morbidly romantic," she decided. "But are you-?"

"Chloe, stop talking," I told her with a laugh, and then reached out to take her hand. She crawled onto the bed and over top of me as I resituated myself to rest my head on my pillow. Then she looked down at me, biting her lip.

"Okay," she sighed out. "I guess I'll come clean. I'm... kind of still a virgin. In a way."

I stared at her, taken aback. "In a way?" I echoed.

Her cheeks turned a little pink as she explained, "I was fourteen, and there was, like, three minutes of fumbling around at a sleepover. I don't think that actually counts."

"That makes me feel so much better," I breathed out, and felt some of the tension dissipate as she hung her head and I chuckled. "Like, a hundred times better."

She raised her head to sigh at me. "But you're still nervous, right?"

I stopped smiling and nodded. "Yeah."

"Good. Because I am, too."

"Okay." I reached up to cup her cheek, chewing on the inside of my cheek for a moment, and then suggested, "Just kiss me?"

"Okay," she echoed, and leaned down to do just

that.

And once we'd started kissing, the rest was surprisingly easy. There was an awkward moment where my pants got stuck around my ankles and another when I couldn't unhook Chloe's bra as fast as expected, but that was okay. We laughed it off and it wasn't an issue. Sex was hyped as this massive, life-changing experience, but I didn't feel any differently afterward. Just more attached to Chloe, if that was even possible, and maybe a little more prone to let an "I love you" slip out any day now.

And just more scared to lose her.

Chapter Eleven

Chloe was still in my bed when my dad and Deborah got home later that night. She was asleep, but I was alert enough to hear their voices carry upstairs.

"I'm just gonna go check on Harper really quick," I heard Dad say, and my eyes immediately widened.

"Shit," I hissed, realizing there was no way I'd be able to wake Chloe and hide her fast enough. I could already hear his footsteps on the stairs.

"Honey, she's probably asleep. Check on her tomorrow?" came Deborah's voice.

There was a pause in Dad's footsteps.

Deborah spoke again. "She'll be fine."

The footsteps resumed, but I realized with relief that they were heading back downstairs. We were safe as long Chloe could get back home by morning.

She managed it, but only after being unable to find her shoes and then sneaking out barefoot through the back door early in the morning, which was further from my dad's bedroom than the front. I saw her off and then went back to sleep.

The second time I woke up, it was to a knock on my door. I rubbed at my eyes and sat up, groggily calling out, "Come in!"

To my surprise, it was Deborah, not my dad, who cracked open the door and peered in at me.

"Oh. Hi," I said. My eyes widened when she stuck an arm through the door and I saw what she held: Chloe's shoes.

"Your dad went into the kitchen for a minute when we first got home last night," she explained, very clearly amused. "I wasn't sure he'd recognize that these weren't yours, but I've seen Chloe wearing them, so I took the time to hide them before he saw them. I'm sorry she couldn't find them."

She tossed the shoes into my room, and I stared at her hard for a moment, before simply declaring, "Truce."

She laughed and moved to shut the door. "Okay, Harper."

* * *

The weather in California didn't change over the course of the next few weeks, despite summer drawing closer to its end. Chloe and I spent most of our time outside together, either by the cliff and the

176

water or at the park or even just walking the streets of our neighborhood with Baxter. I didn't want to stay away from her. I couldn't. And luckily, by the time August hit, my dad had accepted that I was growing up and that avoiding discussions about certain uncomfortable topics didn't stop me from growing up, and that Chloe's much less uptight parents were letting me spend the night at their house.

One night, after we'd finally untangled ourselves from each other and agreed to try and go to sleep, Chloe gently traced letters into my back with her finger while I, half-asleep, guessed what she was trying to spell out.

"U... end word. R... end word. P...R...E...T...T..." I spelled out, before laughing quietly and saying, "Aw, thank you. You're pretty, too."

"You're too good at this. I was going to say 'you're pretty annoying', by the way, but you didn't let me finish."

"Oh, I thought you were going for 'you're pretty but not as pretty as me'. I gave you too much credit."

She chuckled against my shoulder as she leaned in to kiss it. "Okay. Pay attention for this one."

"I will," I yawned out, and focused on the light touches against my back. "I... end word. L...O..." I paused, and then rolled over to face her. She offered me a gentle smile.

"Me too," I told her.

She arched an eyebrow, her demeanor changing

177

instantaneously. "You love chocolate? I thought you were allergic."

"That wasn't what you were going to spell out," I said.

"No," she agreed, leaning in to kiss me. "It wasn't."

* * *

"Maybe this is a weird call to be making," said Robbie over the phone just a few days later.

Confused, I held the phone to my ear with one hand as Chloe painted the nails of my other. I was sitting in my bedroom on the edge of my bed, and Chloe sat on her knees in front of me.

He continued, "I, uh... guess maybe I'm being contradictory here, but I know we haven't seen each other much in the past couple of weeks, and so I just wanted you to know that I get why, and that I don't mind. So just know that it's okay and I get why you're spending all of your time with Chloe."

I laughed lightly. "This is totally a weird call for you to be making. But that's okay. I think it's sweet."

Chloe arched an eyebrow at me and I mouthed, "Robbie." She nodded her understanding and went back to painting my nails.

Robbie sighed on the other end. "Yeah, I'm lame. Okay. Just let me know if you need anything. If anything, uh... happens."

"I will. Seriously, thank you."

"No problem."

I hung up the phone to a questioning look from Chloe as she requested, "Can I ask you something?"

"What's up?" I offered her my other hand as she finished up with the thumbnail of my first.

"You and Robbie are really close. I like him, but I guess I don't really see what you guys have in common."

"We're both very cynical," I offered evasively.

"You both lost someone important to you, I know. I just never thought that was enough to bring two people together like that. Especially since you're so different. He's a lot older, too. Do you guys have some, like, secret dorky hobby you share that you're too embarrassed to tell me about?"

"Yes," I told her, and she laughed.

"Seriously, though."

"Seriously," I confirmed. "I'll never tell you."

"I can't tell if you're messing with me or not right now, but if you're being serious, you'll have to tell me eventually," she pointed out.

"I couldn't. You wouldn't believe me if I did." I resolved to change the subject as soon as the words were out of my mouth. It ached to talk about this.

"Now I know you're messing with me," Chloe confirmed with a shake of your head. "Alright, lesson learned. I accept your strange, seemingly random friendship. I'm just gonna assume he got you into Dungeons and Dragons or something and you're too embarrassed to tell me. It's okay; I wouldn't judge."

"And you shouldn't. You mocked our comic

books but I saw a manga in your closet the other day."

"I was thirteen and it was lesbian-themed," she shot back. "Doesn't count. And it's not the same thing, anyway."

"I bet you still go back and read it."

"Do not."

"Also, I was only reading *Batwoman*. She's a lesbian."

She looked up sharply. "Wait, really? That's a thing?"

"Yeah. There was this whole controversy where she couldn't get married and everything."

"So even Batwoman falls victim to homophobia? That's depressing; I don't wanna read that."

"*Anyway*, Robbie's cool and he gave me *Batwoman* to read for the lesbian content. That should show you what kind of guy he is."

"Does he read manga?" she asked me, and I burst into laughter.

"You have *zero* room to judge now!"

"Shut up. Give me your foot; I'm giving you pink toenails, too."

I grinned down at her as she grabbed my foot and went to work. We sat in comfortable silence for a moment, and I shifted slightly on my bed and let out a soft sigh.

"So how do you feel about a laser tag rematch?" she proposed without warning.

I laughed, surprised. "Really?"

"What, don't think I can beat you? We can do it

just the two of us. One on one."

"Uh huh. I would *crush* you."

"We'll see." She winked at me. "We'll go tomorrow."

"You're serious?"

"Yeah. I liked it. The whole place, actually. I might go back there for my birthday in three weeks, too. You think they let people make reservations? Eh, I'll ask Robbie next time I see him. He probably knows."

"You're having a party?" I forced myself to ask. "Do you know anyone else around here?"

She glared at me as though she was offended, but I could tell she didn't mean it. "Well, I know your family and mine and I know Robbie. It can be small. Plus, can't you totally see my dad getting into laser tag? He'd have a blast."

"It could be fun," I relented, mostly so she would change the subject again. "So maybe tomorrow you could come over after laser tag and stay the night. Dad mentioned leaving tomorrow evening to go somewhere with Deborah for the weekend."

"Oh? Where?"

"I don't know," I admitted. "San Andreas or something?"

"I, uh... I'm not from California, so maybe you know better, but I'm pretty sure that isn't actually a place people go. Like, it might even actually just be fictional. From Grand Theft Auto." She looked like she was trying not to laugh.

"Well, whatever. San *something*. I think. It started

with an 'S'. San Diego? Maybe Sacramento? I wasn't paying attention when he mentioned it. It was while we were texting yesterday morning about your shopping trip with your mom."

"Ha! That's awkward. He didn't see the bikini pics I sent, did he?"

"If he had, you would *not* be in here right now."

"Maybe. He's been letting you off the leash lately. I think my parents have been a good influence on him," she joked. "He doesn't look horrified when he sees us heading upstairs together anymore, at least." She finished up with the last of my toenails and put the nail polish away. I wiggled my toes and made a move to stand, but she made a noise of displeasure and pressed a hand to my chest to keep me on the bed.

"They're not dry enough." She moved to sit next to me and carefully took my hand into hers, admiring my nails as she intertwined our fingers. Before she'd done my nails, she'd painted her own a deep purple color. "You have stubby thumbs," she remarked. "They're cute."

"Your pinkies are crooked," I said. She waited for me to say more, and when I didn't, she laughed and bumped my shoulder with her own.

"Bitch! At least I was nice!"

"Well, they *are*."

* * *

Chloe went into the smoky maze before I did, laser gun in her hand and lights flashing from her vest.

"You have twenty minutes, beginning now," said the young, pimply teenager working the laser tag shift today, and I accepted a gun from him and ducked into the maze, my own vest flashing for a moment before it went dark.

I crouched as I made my way through the maze, squinting through the fog all the while for signs of movement. I could remember my first time in the maze with Chloe like it was yesterday, and stifled a laugh at the mental image of her running wildly through the fog, lights on her vest flashing. I'd thought she was adorable, then, even though I hadn't wanted to.

She was playing differently this time.

I ducked around a corner and was met with the sounds of laser-fire. Chloe had been waiting for me at the other end of the hallway. My vest lit up and I folded my arms across my chest as she pointed and laughed at me.

"Chloe one, Harper nothing!"

"You know, us hardcore gamers have a word for what you just did, and it isn't a complimentary term," I informed her. She just laughed at me again and ran off.

A few seconds later, my lights stopped flashing and I took off after her, winding through the hallways without regard for how much noise I was making.

I found Chloe hiding behind a smaller wall before she could make sense of where I was, and mashed my gun right into her vest as I pulled the trigger over and over again. "Die, cretin!"

"That's not very nice," was all she said, but she was grinning at me as she stood. "You're so cute when you get into this nerdy stuff, though." She leaned in and kissed me for a moment as the lights on her vest flashed, her gun momentarily disabled. Then the lights stopped and I beat her to firing. She groaned as her vest started flashing all over again.

"Nice try," I told her, pecking her on the lips once more, and then ran off before she could use her gun again.

"It almost worked!" she called after me.

We spent the next ten minutes running around through the fog, shooting at and teasing each other when we'd find ourselves in the same area. I was sweating by the time we were nearly done, and I was also, frankly, destroying Chloe. She'd only managed to hit me twice more since shooting me that first time after I'd just entered the maze.

I found myself hiding back in one of the corner bases for the last couple of minutes, using the elevation to search for Chloe, who was nowhere to be found. For a moment, standing there in the total silence, I began to get worried. Would something happen to her in the maze? It was unlikely, but with three weeks until her birthday, I was paranoid.

But before that paranoia could manifest itself into outright panic, I felt a gun press into the back of my vest. I let out a laugh, mostly relieved. "I can't believe you snuck in here without me noticing."

"Drop the gun and put your hands where I can see them," she joked. I tried to spin around and she immediately shot me, then grinned at me when we were face to face.

"Okay, so you got, like, four points. I still kicked your ass."

"I improved. I said I'd get better, remember?"

"I actually only remember you telling me to 'lose the boy'," I admitted.

"Well, that too. It was fun without him."

"I like Robbie."

"Yeah, but you like me better." Grinning, she leaned in to kiss me. I pressed my gun to her vest and pulled the trigger again just as the voice over the intercom told us our game was over. Chloe let her gun fall from her hands and laughed into my mouth even as she wrapped her arms around me and pulled me closer. "Overly competitive nerd."

* * *

I drove us home after we stopped nearby for some fast food, and Chloe stared out of her window for the better part of the trip. We'd had a fun day, but a part of me felt a little uneasy. I knew why.

Finally she asked, "Do you think every teenager in a relationship daydreams about getting married, and buying a house, and having pets or kids or *both,* and makes up names for them and all that dumb stuff, or am I just lame?"

"I don't think about it," I admitted, and then added when she turned and stared at me, "I mean,

I'd like all of that, but nothing's a guarantee in life and I don't want to get my hopes up."

"I just wonder if those ninety-eight percent of teenage couples who'll break up at some point *know* that they're part of the ninety-eight percent. Like, do they sit around and go 'eh, this is nice for now', or do they actually have these embarrassing images of their future only to have it all destroyed in the end?"

I shot her a strange look. "That's... Why on earth would you think about that?"

"Well, it'd be nice to know that the fact that I think about our future is some sort of indication that it might all come true. Like maybe it's some sort of sign that we're gonna be a thing for a long time."

"I don't think most people assume a relationship is doomed. Especially not teenagers. Most of us naively think we'll never break up and that everything will go perfectly fine and we'll get married and live happily ever after."

"'Naively?' Harsh." She turned away, and I could tell I'd hurt her feelings.

"I don't mean it like that, Chloe. It's just... it's like you said. Ninety-eight percent of the time that's not how it happens. Doesn't that make it naïve to think you're part of the two percent?"

"Well, if I'm the only one who bothers acting like we could be, I guess it does," she said, her tone clipped.

I sighed quietly, forcing myself to keep my eyes on the road. "I'd marry you, Chloe. I've told you that. I meant it."

"Then how do you not think about it?"

"Because I don't want to think about something I might not ever have," I shot back, with more force than I'd intended. The tension was palpable after I'd fallen silent.

"I was just trying to find a way to let you know that I think about having a life with you, is all," Chloe mumbled at last. "Even if it seems naïve and stupid and even though we're just teenagers and it's only been a few weeks and we don't know for sure how long this will last. I thought if you knew *I* thought about the future maybe you'd let yourself do the same. I thought maybe I could change the way you think about life."

"You have," I insisted. "Since we've met, you've changed a lot of things about me. But you can't make everything better just by existing. Especially given that we can't even control how long we're around."

"I don't believe that. We all have a choice. I can't believe everything's pointless like you seem to sometimes."

"Okay. You win. You've changed my mind."

There was a long silence, and out of the corner of my eye, I saw Chloe fold her arms across her chest. "Don't be petulant," she mumbled. "It's just exhausting to be around all the time, you know? You smile a lot around me but sometimes I get the feeling you're holding back. Like if you enjoy life too much you might forget to hate it." She sighed and shook her head. "I shouldn't have brought it up."

"What do you want? For me to say that I think about what kind of house we'd live in or what we'd name a dog? I don't. I'm busy trying to get through every day."

"Why does every day have to be some massive struggle? Why can't you just enjoy it for what it is?"

"If you're just with me because you want to fix me, you're wasting your time. You have to accept that this isn't going to change."

"You think I'm that kind of person. Good to know."

We pulled into my driveway and I sighed as I shut my car off. My phone buzzed as Chloe moved to get out of the car. "Wait," I told her even as I looked at the message from my dad: *Got a suitcase packed for this weekend?*

I paused, confused. I was going with my dad and Deborah? I'd thought it was just meant to be the two of them.

"Look, I'll be home if you wanna hang out tomorrow," Chloe mumbled, already backing away me. She wouldn't look me in the eyes. "Let me know if you're not too busy sadly pondering the futility of human existence or whatever. Sorry I *dared* to think of being happy one day."

"Wait," I sighed out again, and walked to her when she grudgingly paused. I bit my lip and closed my eyes, then let out a sharp breath and tried to relax. "I'm just scared to lose you, is all. I don't want to think about the future because I can't think about how perfect it could be without thinking about how it'd feel to lose it all." I lowered my eyes, unable to look into hers as I lied, "Maybe that'll change, but if it doesn't, you have to be okay with it."

"When does it end? When do you accept that you could be happy? When you're married? When you have three dogs and financial stability and a job you enjoy and everything else people are meant to want out of life?"

"I don't know." I still didn't look at her. "Maybe... ask me again in a month. Okay?"

"Okay, then. I will." She said it like she was accepting a challenge. "Thirty days from today."

"Okay." I felt lower than dirt for even suggesting it in the first place, and for a moment, I was sure I was going to start crying.

The front door opened behind me and my dad popped his head out. "Hey, Harper, I checked your room; you forgot to pack?"

I turned around and sighed, "I didn't know I was going, Dad. I'm really not in the mood."

"Deborah's got a business conference at a resort in Sacramento and she's been gracious enough to make sure we got a room all three of us can stay in. There's a pool there and a restaurant she's been dying to show the both of us. She grew up there. I *told* you all of this. She's going to be here soon and I won't let you back out; it's extremely rude."

"I don't want to go," I repeated. "I'll stay at Chloe's."

"I don't think so," Dad insisted.

Behind me, Chloe nudged me and added, "Go, Harper. Maybe we need a break. We can talk on Monday."

"I don't want a break. I-" I trailed off, feeling tears prick at the corners of my eyes again. I felt so hopeless. Chloe was upset and I couldn't tell her why I felt the way I did, and my dad was going to make me leave her *while* she was upset and with three weeks to go until her birthday, and I didn't know what to say to either of them to make things better. "I just want everything to be okay with us. I don't want you to be mad at me; I just always say the wrong thing and I know I'm hard to be around sometimes. Please don't be mad."

I said this all to Chloe, visibly near tears, and she softened a little and reached out to wipe at my eyes. "I'll text you," she relented. "Okay? All weekend. I'll be right here when you get back."

Even as she said it, the uneasy feeling I'd had all day began to intensify. A heavy knot formed in my stomach. I worried it was same feeling I'd gotten the night my mom had died, and then hated myself for not being able to remember.

I swallowed hard and turned back to my dad. "I'm staying here."

Dad reached up to rub at his temples, and his jaw clenched with anger. "*Harper*. I have given you all the freedom in the world this summer. I'm asking you to please take two days to go on a free trip and stay in a free hotel with a free pool and room service. This isn't exactly a chore."

"Just let Chloe come too, then, I can-"

"Harper, go with your dad," Chloe cut in. She stepped around to my front and took my hand in hers. "It sounds like fun. You guys should spend some time together. I hog you enough as it is."

"You don't understand; I can't leave you. If I leave you..." I trailed off and closed my eyes, realizing how crazy I must've sounded. But I knew – I *knew* – that this ache I felt wasn't there for no reason.

There were a lot of things I'd come to know that summer. That fate was unchangeable. That Chloe's death was coming no matter what I did. That I had to accept those things because I'd drive myself crazy if I didn't.

But that didn't make it any less impossible to just let go. I wasn't ready. I wasn't *ever* going to be ready.

"Can you just-" I choked out, and saw Chloe's alarmed reaction to the tears that came rolling down my cheeks without warning. "Can you be safe?"

"It's just a weekend," she repeated. "I don't understand." But she reached out to wipe at my eyes again.

"Harper, this is a little ridiculous," said my dad, who'd slipped out of the front door to join us now. "If leaving for two days is this upsetting, you two definitely need some time apart."

"It's just been a rough d-" Chloe started to say, and then seemed to change her mind when she realized that we'd actually had a perfectly fine day together. "We argued in the car, is all," she said instead.

"I'm sorry to hear that, but you'll have plenty of time to patch things up later. Right now Harper needs to come pack her bag; Deborah's going to be here any minute now and I'd rather she not find out Harper didn't want to go. It'd really hurt her feelings. Harper can call you later, Chloe."

"Okay. I can go." Chloe stepped away from me and I shook my head, my vision blurry.

"Wait. I'll go in, Dad, just let me say goodbye."

Dad sighed as I wiped at my eyes again, but I saw him soften. He reached out to pat me on the shoulder. "Alright, but please hurry."

"I will."

He left to head back inside, and Chloe, shooting me a sympathetic look, leaned in to give me a hug. I knew the second Dad was gone that I was going to lose it. I was trembling and as Chloe squeezed me tight, I cried into her shoulder. I knew I had to look absolutely insane to her then; she had no way of understanding why I was so upset.

"I don't know what I said, but I'm sorry," she murmured. "I shouldn't get mad at you for being a little pessimistic. I can't blame you after what you've been through."

"It's not your fault," I sobbed out. "I'm sorry I've been awful. I'm sorry I didn't smile enough and that I wouldn't ride roller coasters with you and that I didn't let you kiss me that first weekend when I knew I liked you too. I was just scared."

"I get it. I know." She squeezed me tighter. "It's okay. It's okay that we're different. Maybe that's what makes this whole thing work. You'd be boring if you were just like me."

I pulled away from her and wiped the tears from my cheeks. "You are *not* boring."

"I know. Neither are you. How many people out there have chocolate allergies? That's totally weird and interesting." I forced a small laugh and she smiled at me. "I'm gonna text you nonstop, okay? Because as much as I support you bonding with your dad and his girlfriend, that trip honestly sounds boring as hell. And my weekend will be boring without you. So I'll also be texting you for selfish reasons. I kind of have no other friends."

"I hogged your summer," I said, sniffing.

"Trust me, that was *not* against my will." She pulled me in for another tight hug. "I love you."

"I love you, too." I could feel tears welling up in my eyes again, and struggled to fight them off. She pulled away from me just enough to kiss me.

It was the hardest thing I'd ever done in my life to pull away from her and walk away, but I did it. I walked backwards for the first few steps, eyes on her as she smiled at me and gave me a small wave goodbye. I glanced up at her forehead, felt myself fall apart all over again at the sight of the sixteen that still rested there, and then looked back down into her eyes. It was the first part of her I'd ever seen, and I wanted it to be the last, too, if this was

193

the end for us.

Then I turned around and went inside, climbed up the stairs to my room, and broke down as I began to pack my bag, muffling my sobs with my arm as my vision began to blur all over again.

Chapter Twelve

I texted Robbie in the car as Deborah drove, feeling numb all over as I forced my thumbs to spell out my message. *"I think it's this weekend. Dad made me go to Sacramento with him. I feel so helpless."*

I leaned my head against the window and stared at the back of the seat in front of me. We were in Deborah's car. There was a fitness magazine that rested in the pocket on the back of the seat. My phone buzzed as I stared blankly at the cover. I looked down at Robbie's message.

"I'm here."

I felt empty, and I knew it was from more than

just the thought of losing Chloe. Dad was starting a new life with his girlfriend. He was happy, and I couldn't ruin that. I wouldn't let myself lean on him again; he'd done enough for me over the past four years.

Robbie remained the sole person who knew and understood what I was going through. After Chloe was gone, he was all I'd really have. I wasn't sure that'd be enough for me. I had nothing left to feel for anyone after Chloe was gone. She'd owned all of my heart, and I'd let her have it. I'd put down my walls long enough to let her invade and take over completely, even though I'd known all along that this was how it was going to end. I felt so stupid now, and I wondered what part of me had let myself be convinced that it was okay to fall for Chloe.

And I wondered what awful thing I'd done in a past life to deserve the one I had now.

* * *

After we'd settled into our hotel room in Sacramento that evening, Deborah and my dad insisted on going out to dinner. I'd requested that Chloe check in every hour or so, but Dad made me put up my phone for dinner.

I knew it was clear to them that I was distracted. I ate my food in silence, and could barely get it down. There was a lump in my throat that wouldn't go away.

Deborah said something about it first, which surprised me. "Harper, are you alright? You seem quiet."

"She's got some relationship troubles," Dad answered for me, shooting me a sympathetic smile and placing a hand on my shoulder. "She and Chloe had a little spat right before we left."

"Oh." Deborah looked taken aback. "I'm sorry to hear that. It wouldn't have bothered me if you'd have wanted to stay back to patch things up with Chloe."

"Oh, no, I wanted her to come," Dad explained. "I think the change in scenery will be good for her, even if it's for just a couple of days. She can talk to Chloe when she gets back."

Deborah still looked dubious. Fed up, I reached down into my pants pocket and took out my phone. Dad sighed at me.

"Harper, we're having dinner."

"I don't care," I shot back, and promptly stood up and left the table.

I wound through the crowded restaurant until I was back by the front door. Outside, there were several benches where customers could sit while waiting to be seated. I found the most isolated bench and sat down, then checked my phone. No new texts from Chloe. I immediately dialed her number and closed my eyes, murmuring a silent prayer to whatever was up in the sky that she'd pick up.

She didn't. I set my phone down beside me and slouched forward, my head in my hands. I felt like I couldn't breathe.

My phone buzzed beside me and I snatched at it. It was Chloe: *"In shower, call u 2nite."*

I let out a heavy breath and pocketed my phone. The front door to the restaurant swung open and it wasn't Dad who emerged, but Deborah. She looked around for a moment before spotting me, and I prepared for an uncomfortable conversation as she headed toward me.

"Mind if I sit?" she asked. I shrugged my shoulders, and she joined me on the bench.

"Bet Dad's pissed," I mumbled. "Is that why he sent you?"

"He didn't send me," she admitted. "I asked him to let me talk to you. I think maybe it's a little hard to talk about your relationships with your own parent. Especially a dad, as his daughter."

"I don't know you very well," I reminded her quietly. "Why bother? You and my dad haven't even been dating for that long."

"That's true. But I do like him." She paused, and then leaned back against the bench. I could feel her gaze on the side of my face, but kept my own eyes on my lap. "I'm sorry he made you come here for the weekend. I remember what it was like to be a teenage girl. The person you're dating sort of becomes your whole world."

"Don't say it like that," I countered. "Like it's this immature teenage thing and like it's a phase that'll pass. Besides, I'm not upset because of some dumb fight."

She fell silent at that for a moment. "...Well,

would you like to talk about what's upsetting you?"

"You wouldn't understand."

She let out a light laugh. "Oh, honey, I think I'd understand a whole lot better than you'd think. Like I said: I've been a teenage girl before."

"Did you lose a mother when you were twelve, too?" I snapped, and she was quiet again.

"No," she admitted at last. "But I did lose my husband. I know the pain never quite goes away. And sometimes it shows up when you least expect it to."

"Do you ever get afraid you'll lose someone again?" I asked, gaze still on my lap. I was stiff and unmoving and it still felt impossible to swallow. Even speaking didn't feel natural; it was like every syllable had to be pushed from my throat.

"That's a tough question," said Deborah. "I think..." She trailed off, and then let out a sigh. "You know, I think feeling that kind of pain again is utterly terrifying. But I think a big part of healing is coming to terms with the fact that it's a part of life, and that while it does hurt, it doesn't outweigh the good times we got to share with that person before their death."

"That's what everyone keeps saying," I told her. "I don't understand why. I don't remember my mother very much anymore." I felt tears prick at the corners of my eyes and struggled to fight them off. "All I can think about is losing the people I care about. I... I don't want to lose Chloe. I don't want to forget her."

"Harper, Chloe seems to really like you. I don't

think she's going anywhere, and I'm sure she's safe at home."

I shook my head. "I knew when it happened to Mom. I got this feeling... and I was right. And I think I have it again. I need to be with her. I know you have your business stuff but I'm not okay being here right now. When it happened with Mom I didn't trust it and I'm not making that mistake again. Even if I can't stop it, I just want to be there."

I wiped at the tears on my cheeks and finally turned to Deborah, who was watching me with furrowed eyebrows. I noticed, with muted surprise, that one of her hands had moved to rest against her stomach. She let out a deep breath, and then nodded once, shortly.

"Then let's go."

Both of my eyebrows shot up. "What? Really?"

"Of course. My meeting isn't until tomorrow afternoon. The drive is short enough. If it'll help you feel better, we'll go."

"What's going on?" That was Dad, who'd walked outside and approached us just in time to hear Deborah's offer. "Deb, you don't have to-"

"I want to," Deborah insisted. "She doesn't feel well. I'll take her home; you can just hold the hotel room for me and I'll be back tonight."

"Deb, you don't have to do that."

"I want to," Deborah repeated. She stood, already digging into her purse for her car keys. "Harper, you don't need your suitcase, do you?"

I shook my head quickly, hardly daring to believe

this was actually happening. "No, it can come back with you guys on Sunday."

"Deb," Dad tried to interrupt, but when he saw she wasn't changing her mind, he said instead, "You need a good night's sleep. I'll take her back."

"Will you?" I challenged him, uncertain.

"I don't like it," Dad told me, "and I think you're very lucky Deborah's being so nice to you. But if she's okay with you going back, I'd rather take you back myself than ask her to make the drive." He glanced over his shoulder with a disappointed shake of his head. "Let me go pay the bill and we'll leave."

He turned to head back into the restaurant, and Deborah offered me a small smile.

"Thank you," I told her, still a little stunned.

"Say hello to Chloe for me," she replied simply. "She's a very sweet girl."

"I will. Thank you. I will."

* * *

It would be a two-hour drive back to San Francisco at most; at least, an hour and a half. Dad was tense beside me in the driver's seat, but he was the furthest thing from my mind.

I checked the clock on my phone. It was almost eight. I hadn't heard from Chloe in nearly an hour.

I scrolled through my contact list until I reached her number, pressed it, and then lifted the phone to my ear. As it rang, I closed my eyes and murmured a quiet plea to whatever was doing this to her that it'd hold off for just a little while longer. I wanted to see her again. I needed to.

"Hey, Harper. How's the hotel?"

I let out a sigh of relief, but struggled with an answer. Chloe sounded a little sleepy, and even as I opened my mouth to respond, I heard her let out a yawn.

"It's good," I said at last. "Are you about to sleep?" Maybe I'd come over and join her for the night. Surprise her.

"Yep. Laser tag wore me out; you have no idea."

"So you're not doing anything?"

"Nah. Might put on a movie or something until I fall asleep, but that's it. What about you?"

"Um, I don't know. You're really not leaving the house?"

She sounded a little amused when she replied. "Not unless my parents have some sort of surprise trip waiting for me. They're downstairs watching TV right now, though, so that seems pretty unlikely. Are you feeling any better?"

"Yes," I lied. "I just miss you."

"I miss you too. But your dad's probably right. We've been attached at the hip. A few days apart won't hurt."

My heart sank, and I began to reconsider showing up at her house. If she really was just going to go to sleep for the night soon, then maybe I had more time, anyway. Maybe I had another day. At this point, another day felt like another lifetime.

"You're not still upset with me for today, are you?" I asked her.

"Of course not. I guess I just... think it's kind of sad, you know? You don't deserve what happened to you, and it's so sad that it's changed you so much. That doesn't mean I don't adore who you are, but I just want to see you happy."

"You make me happy," I told her. "So just... just stick around, okay?"

"That's the plan. Stick around, you graduate, I graduate, we go to colleges that are close by-"

"Or to the same one," I suggested.

"Exactly. We'll room together after I get there. I'll join a sorority and then quit when I get tired of having to bring boys to date nights; you'll have taken a ton of Philosophy classes your freshman year and you'll annoy the hell out of me. Livin' the dream."

"Philosophy is Robbie's thing," I corrected, unable to stop the corners of my lips from curling up despite myself. "I think I'd hate it."

"Well, you'd take Intro to Video Games or something dumb like that, then. Does that exist? Anyway, then you graduate and get your degree in...?"

I paused, uncertain. I had no idea what major I was interested in. But I wanted to play along for her. "How about... Computer Science?"

"Okay, so you get a Computer Science degree and become like this world class hacker, but like a legit one that gets hired by companies to try and hack into their systems to test their security. My dad knew a guy who did that. And I'll get a Finance degree so that when you inevitably go rogue and illegally hack millions of dollars into our joint bank account, I know how to keep it safe and how to invest it while we're on the run."

"With our two children named Bonnie and Clyde," I added, and she let out a laugh.

"Yes! Perfect. And our dog. No! Wait. One of those overly fluffy white cats that always sits on the main villain's lap in cheesy movies. We'll name it Mr. Piddles as an homage to Dana Fairbanks from The L Word."

"Baxter has to come, too."

"He'll be old by then, so he might slow us down. Don't want dead weight with us when getting caught means that Bonnie and Clyde will be left in foster care with no money."

"Leave them some in an offshore untraceable bank account somewhere."

"I like the way you think," she said, laughing again, and we fell into a comfortable silence.

"Something tells me it wouldn't actually go that way," I said at last. "But it's nice to imagine it anyway."

"The real version would involve a lot less crime and a lot more boring domesticity. But I have a feeling it'd somehow be even better."

"We can only hope," I said, my smile gone by now.

"It's not so bad, is it? Hoping?" she asked me. "What's life without something to hope for?"

I closed my eyes, phone still pressed to my ear.

"You're right. You've always been right."

"You're a good girlfriend, Harper." I could hear the smile in her voice, and the sleepiness. She yawned again. "Well, I should probably get some shut-eye. Text me tomorrow? Bright and early, before you get distracted by the free resort pool?"

"Okay. I will." I didn't want her to go, but I knew I couldn't keep her on the phone forever. "Every hour again."

"Sounds perfect. I love you, Harper."

"I love you too, Chloe."

The call ended with a click, but I kept the phone against my ear. I felt like crying all over again.

Dad was still oozing tension beside me, but it dissipated somewhat when he heard me sniff.

"It was just one weekend, Harper," he sighed out. "It would've been fine."

I didn't have the willpower to argue with him. I couldn't.

We drove on, and I stared down at my phone as the minutes ticked by. Eight thirty passed. Then nine o'clock. Then nine thirty.

Our drive progressed in complete silence. I felt the pressure in my stomach build, and my heart was pounding like it had right before the drop on the roller coaster Chloe'd forced me onto. I scrolled through photos on my phone, my ears ringing. We'd taken so many over the summer.

I settled on one of the two of us by the lake and stared. I looked distracted in the picture because I'd been taking it. Chloe was kissing my cheek. I swallowed hard.

At just past nine forty-five, we turned into our neighborhood and drove down the winding road that housed both my place and Chloe's. I forced myself to look up. I saw the blue lights before Dad did.

"What the...?" he murmured next to me. His car slowed to a stop in front of a crowd of our neighbors. They stood near three police cars, directly in front of Chloe's house. A teenage boy who looked absolutely distraught and a mother who clutched him like he'd break if she let go were standing between a four-door car with a shattered windshield and the crowd, but Chloe and her parents weren't there.

The first tears swelled in my eyes and began to spill down my cheeks, and, completely numb, I flung open the passenger's side door with my seatbelt still on and vomited out onto the street.

Chapter Thirteen

I sat in the car while Dad got out to go talk to our neighbors. I felt incapable of doing anything other than staring straight ahead. My body wouldn't react to my head, and my head couldn't form coherent thoughts. I managed to glance down at my phone and saw the hand clutching it was trembling. Chloe's picture was still up, and I let my phone slip through my fingers and onto the floor in front of my seat. Then I raised my hand to my mouth and let out a sob.

That was how Dad found me when he came back to the car. He got in without saying anything, immediately slammed the door shut, and threw the car into reverse. Seconds later, we were speeding out of the neighborhood. I didn't know where we were going. I couldn't think.

"It'll be okay, honey," he said to me, as though that was supposed to mean anything to me. I already knew it wouldn't be okay. I'd known it wouldn't be okay from the moment I'd met Chloe.

I found the strength to retrieve my phone somehow. I'd thought of Robbie. I sent him a text that I wouldn't remember sending later. There were misspellings, but I'd meant to say "hospital". I knew without Dad having to tell me that that was where we'd be going.

He let me know I was correct sometime later, while we were still on our way, though not directly. He called Deborah. His voice was shaking, but I picked out bits and pieces. "Accident." "Headed to hospital." "Only ten minutes ago."

He hung up and took my hand in his. His palm was clammy and he was trembling. I knew I was, too, but I couldn't feel it. I felt like I was watching all of it happen to someone else. I no longer felt like throwing up because I could feel myself shutting down. I didn't want to feel what I'd felt when I was twelve again. I didn't want to ever feel anything at all again.

We parked near the emergency room at the hospital. Dad turned the keys and shut the car off, but left them in the ignition, he was so distracted. He hurried over to my side of the car and opened my door, then leaned over me to unbuckle my seatbelt when I didn't move. When I still didn't get out of the car, he knelt next to me and took my hand again. "Harper, look at me. She'll be alright."

I pressed my lips together and felt more tears come. I hadn't realized I'd had any hope left at all until he confirmed right to my face that it was Chloe.

"I don't want to go in," I tried to say, but my mouth wouldn't move. Dad kept urging me on, but he was speaking faster than my brain could process.

"Harper, please. Harper," he kept saying, until at last he gripped the car door and pressed his forehead to it, squeezing his eyes shut tightly. "Harper, we have to be there."

I recognized those words. I hadn't wanted to go inside with Mom, either. I wondered if he was thinking of her now. If this was even about the girl I loved for him, or if he was just reliving losing the girl *he* loved.

I turned and slipped out of the car, then stood on shaky legs. Dad collected himself and helped me walk across the parking lot. I'm not sure how I stayed up, but I did.

Chloe's mother and father were alone in the lobby, clutching each other. I saw her father's hands before I could look away, and knew instinctively that this was the moment I'd see over and over again, every night when I closed my eyes. His hands were stained with dried blood.

My stomach started working again and I stumbled to the nearest garbage can to wretch for the second time. Dad was there, at my back, and then Chloe's parents were looking at us, their cheeks stained with tears even worse than my own were.

"There's no news yet," was all her dad could muster up the energy to say. I was glad he seemed unable to spare us any more detail. I couldn't know any more about what had happened. I didn't want details. Ever.

We waited there for what felt like hours for good news I knew wouldn't come. I thought of all the things I hadn't done right. I wished I'd given her everything she'd wanted from the very beginning. I'd conquer every fear I had now just to see her smile.

A nurse came to take Chloe's parents away to a different waiting room sometime later. I learned that Chloe was in surgery, then, and wished I hadn't.

Robbie found us not long after that. He didn't know what to say any more than my dad did. He sat beside me in one of the chairs, ran a hand through his hair, and then placed his face in his hands. Maybe later on I'd just appreciate that he'd been there, but I didn't then. Dad paced back and forth not far from us.

There were people in and out as we waited, but I didn't look at any of them. I pulled my knees up to my chest, eventually, and pressed my face against them, closing my eyes and swallowing back more nausea. I thought I'd be more angry at myself than I was, but it wasn't me I was angry at. I was just angry that things were the way they were, and I didn't know how to focus that. How could I be angry at a force? How could I let that out?

I squeezed my eyes shut tighter and mumbled to Robbie, "Everything's pointless. *Everything.*"

He turned his head to face me, and then shook it. "No."

I pulled back to stare at him, stony-faced. "This wasn't worth it."

"It just feels that way now," he told me. He was quiet, but I sensed it was because he was worried he was upsetting me. And he was.

I swallowed hard, all too aware the tears were going to come again. "My girlfriend is in another room dying-" I stopped, choking on the word, and then stood. I needed to get out.

"Harper?" Dad called out from across the room when he noticed me heading for the door. "Harper-!"

"I need some air," I managed to say, and when I glanced back and saw him starting after me and Robbie getting to his feet, I turned away and sprinted.

I was faster than Robbie, I knew, and Dad was too far away to catch me before I got to his car. I clambered in and shut the door behind me, then locked the doors and started the car up with the keys he'd left in the ignition. Robbie reached me before Dad and yanked at the door handle, then banged on the window.

"Harper!" His voice was muffled. "Harper, don't do this."

I didn't even look at him; just shifted the gear into drive and then pealed out of the parking lot, tires squealing. Behind me, I saw Robbie rush for his car. My phone rang and I ignored it.

I wasn't sure where I was going at first. I just knew that I didn't want to be around when the bad news came. I couldn't take another second in a waiting room when I already knew what I was waiting to hear. Why bother? Why bother with anything if this was always going to be the result? Every life ended with a group of hysterical people in a waiting room. Hell, life *itself* could be measured in how many times we'd stood in a hospital room and waited for bad news. I didn't know the number on my forehead – the one that told me how long in years I'd be around – but I had a second number that could tell me how long I'd *been* around. Long enough to outlive two loved ones. Long *enough.*

In the end, we'd all just wind up being reduced to a number one way or another, and no amount of emotional attachment could change that. Even a person like Chloe was only going to live on as a memory. The memories would fade, and we'd age, and soon there would be no one left who knew her. My mother had been fading for years now, and there was nothing I could do to stop it. All I wanted was some semblance of power. Just some sign that I had some control. That was all I'd ever wanted.

I wound up at the place my parents had used to go to be alone when they'd been younger. Where Chloe and I'd had our first kiss.

I left the water alone and stopped by the cliff, then sat down on the grass just a few feet from the edge. I wondered about my own number. I wondered if it was 20, or 30, or 40. It wasn't seventeen; that was the only thing I was certain of. The only thing Robbie'd ever confirmed for me. Fate had determined I wasn't going to die tonight.

I stood up and looked over at the cliff's edge again, but before I could even consider moving, I heard footsteps and panting as Robbie approached behind me.

"Harper, don't," he warned, watching me turn to face him. "Don't be stupid."

"How did you know I was here?" I asked him.

"Sped like hell to keep up with you," he breathed out, taking a step toward me. Instinctively, I stepped backward, and he immediately stopped. "*Harper.*"

"I don't want to die," I clarified, glancing over my shoulder. The drop was steep, with rocks at the bottom. There was no way I'd survive it. "But my number isn't seventeen. All I wanted was to know that I could beat the numbers. Maybe this is how I do it."

"That's not how it works, Harper, and you know it," he said. "It might look impossible to survive, but you aren't meant to die tonight, so you won't. No matter what you do."

"That's not true!" I shook my head. "What if I were to get a gun-"

"Then you won't be able to get one. That's not how it works," he repeated. "You're not going anywhere, and as much as it might hurt right now, this isn't the solution."

"How can you say that? After what happened to your sister, how can you say that? They didn't deserve to die." I pressed my lips together and wiped at my eyes, trying to stop myself from crying again. "If we can't beat this, then what's the point?"

"Maybe there is no point. I don't know. But we go on anyway because we have to. There are people who love and care about you. There are experiences you're going to have that you're going to be glad you were around for. And yes, there are going to be things that'll tear you up on the inside and make you wish you'd never been born. That's a part of life. But it's not ever going to be enough to risk your life trying to prove a point. Look at yourself! You're a step away from using yourself to test fate when there's a girl at a hospital who needs you right now. What if she wakes up and she's got another few days? What if she's up right now and she's got an hour left? And you're out here doing this."

I opened my mouth to suck in a breath, feeling my vision go blurry as tears welled up in my eyes again. This time I couldn't stop them from falling. "I don't know how to live with this," I told him. "Not this, too. I thought I was stronger but I'm not."

"You have me. You have your dad. Maybe that can be enough. I know we'll do everything we can to make it enough. Chloe wouldn't-"

"Don't use her," I interrupted. "I don't want you to use her."

"Then..." He hesitated, and then took another step toward me. "Then let us be enough. Your number won't be coming up for a while, Harper. I know we can be enough. Maybe this is as low as you get, and if you can get through this, then you can get through anything. This is a bad start, but give life a chance to prove it's worth it."

"You're too cynical to believe any of that," I shot back. "I know you are."

"Well, maybe I'm starting to. You saw a girl like Chloe and wondered how she could wind up with the life she got. You hoped you were wrong and that somehow she could beat her number. Now give me a chance to hope that this isn't it for you."

"Look at how Chloe turned out," I pointed out. I closed my eyes and tried to keep my voice even. "Look at where she is tonight."

"She might not be gone yet," he said. "Come back to the hospital. Come see this through." He stepped closer and offered his hand to me, and I blinked out a few more tears as I stared. I knew, ultimately, that I couldn't ever step backwards. Not after my mom, and not even after this.

"Okay," I said, and took his hand.

"I'll drive," he replied, and pulled me into him.

* * *

Dad gripped me so tightly when we returned to the hospital that it hurt. "Thank you," I heard him say to Robbie while my face was buried in his chest.

We waited, then I didn't leave the room again. I didn't speak. I closed my eyes and remembered Chloe: every moment of her I could think of. The

215

day we'd met, the afternoons in my room, the trips to get ice cream and play laser tag. I seared it all into my memory. I made sure I'd never let her slip away.

Dad's phone rang several hours later, when my own phone said it was just past four in the morning.

"Thank you," he said as he ended the call, and then he walked to me and Robbie and told us, "That was Kent. The surgeon told them that she's better than when she came in but it still doesn't look good. They're still not sure how she'll do overnight. Kent and Hayley are going to stay but-"

"I want to stay," I demanded immediately. Dad looked like he wanted to protest, but I cut him off. "You would've stayed with Mom."

He fell silent at that. He had no argument for it.

"I'll go pick up some food and some pillows and blankets," Robbie offered.

"I won't eat," I told him, but Dad nodded at him nonetheless.

"Thank you, Robbie."

Robbie left, and Dad took a seat next to me, letting out a deep sigh. After a moment, he opened his mouth to speak.

"You know, when your Mom..." He paused and closed his eyes, letting out a slow exhale. Then he shook his head. "It still hurts to think about, but, um... Eventually you start remembering the good times rather than the one really bad time. And it aches, kind of like a fading bruise, but it doesn't have that sharp sting anymore. If Chloe-"

"I don't think I can do this right now, Dad," I murmured. "I can't."

"Okay," was all he said. He rested his hand on my back and it felt heavy and uncomfortable, but I didn't complain.

"Why do you think bad things happen to good people?" I asked him abruptly.

He took a moment to respond. "I don't know," he said at last. "As cruel as it is, I think it might just be bad luck."

"And you're okay with that? You can go through life every day having accepted that?"

He pat my back once with his hand. "I think I have to be okay with it. And I think that everyone struggles with it. Some people make themselves okay with it by believing that there's a God with a plan, and that good people die because there's something better waiting on the other side. For those of us who don't believe that... We just have to learn to be okay."

* * *

Robbie brought pillows and blankets back, but I didn't fall asleep for a while. None of us did. I paced back and forth instead, restless, and Dad stayed up to watch me, I knew, even if he didn't say it. I knew he was worried I'd leave again, but I didn't plan on it. I was going to see this through to the end, whenever it came.

I curled up in a chair in the corner of the room

eventually and closed my eyes. I didn't believe in a God, I knew, because God was meant to be the epitome of everything good, and I couldn't believe anything completely good was holding the giant magnifying glass given the life I'd had. But I didn't believe anything wholly bad was responsible either. Robbie was probably right. It probably was just fate. But God and the Devil supposedly came with ears, so maybe fate did, too.

"Maybe you're not listening. Maybe you can't listen. But if you can, and you are... you can take whatever you want," I mouthed, my eyes still closed. "Take ten of my years. Take all of them. Just give her more time. She deserves more time. She wants it more than anyone. Give her just a little more time."

* * *

Chloe's parents came to our waiting room around noon the next day. I'd drifted in and out of sleep for a few hours up until then, but as soon as I saw them, I was alert.

Their eyes were red and puffy and their faces were no less tear-streaked than they had been when I'd seen them the night before. But Hayley approached me, offered me a weak smile, and asked, "Would you like to see her?"

I opened and closed my mouth, stunned. "How-?"

"She's in and out of consciousness, but she's stable."

"What?" I shook my head, not daring to believe it.

Was this another drowning? Was she meant to survive this? Was Hayley mistaken; was something going to go wrong?

"We'll wait for her here," Dad cut in, nodding thankfully to Hayley. I got to my feet and followed her. Kent stayed behind.

We wound through hallways and past nurses and beeping machines, and then into the ICU. Hayley led me to the last bed on the right, where a curtain shielded it from view, and then paused and took a deep breath. Then she pulled the curtain aside and let me go in alone.

Chloe was battered and bruised and hooked up to more machines than I thought possible for a single person. I started crying on the spot as I moved to her side, and her eyes fluttered open to look at me. The top of her head was wrapped in bandages; covering everything above her eyes.

She opened her mouth, and, stunned, I realized that she could speak. "Oh, no, don't cry, Harper," she murmured. Her hand stretched out toward me and I took it, careful not to squeeze too tightly. "Don't cry."

I shook my head wordlessly, speechless, and for a minute or so, we didn't speak. I just watched her, tears streaming down my cheeks as her hand squeezed mine.

"Baxter has got to stop slipping his collar and running out in front of cars during his bathroom breaks," she said at last. It was too soon for me to laugh. "He's in big trouble when I get home."

"Did they say you're going to be okay?" I asked her.

She cleared her throat, and then winced. Breathing seemed to be a little difficult for her, and she had a mask over her mouth. She was using her free hand to remove it over and over again when she spoke. "I heard them tell Mom and Dad that I died for a few seconds during surgery. Kid who hit me had a hood ornament that caught me in the lung. Lots of blood in lungs and one collapsed. Then lots of surgery and stitches. Not good. But if I can survive all that, I think I'll be okay." She hesitated, and then joked, "Told you I wasn't going anywhere."

I studied her for a moment, my throat closing up. I didn't dare to be hopeful even as I asked, "Are you allowed to mess with your bandage?"

She let out a slow breath. "I hope so. It's itchy. It'd be great if you could adjust it a bit, actually."

I glanced toward the door to double check that Hayley wasn't coming in, then reached for Chloe's bandage and gently tugged up the left side until her forehead was exposed. The number rested there, clear as day, as though it had been there all along.

84.

Epilogue

Chloe's stay in the hospital was not short. I was back in school before they felt comfortable releasing her. But she did get released, eventually.

In addition to the collapsed lung, she'd had a mild concussion, and she'd broken her leg in too many places to count. Once she was out of the hospital, she had to start physical therapy for that. I immediately began helping as often as I could, between my classes and my new job serving ice cream at the movie theater.

Deborah moved in with me and Dad just a few months after that. I wondered sometimes if she questioned the day I somehow knew I needed to be with Chloe, or if her placing her hand on her stomach had been some kind of indication that she'd felt that same feeling before, too. I knew she couldn't see the numbers, but maybe sensing that something terrible was going to happen to a loved one wasn't something totally exclusive to people like Robbie and me.

Robbie and I continued hanging out at least twice a week. When I wasn't with Chloe, working, or in school, I was usually with him. Ever since I'd stepped away from that cliff, Robbie was more determined than ever to avoid giving me any more details about my number. I supposed I wouldn't know what it was until it was time for me to go. I was surprisingly okay with that.

Seeing Chloe's number change didn't make me gain faith in some sort of benevolent omniscient being, but it did change what it was like to be with her. The dark cloud over our relationship vanished. We spent our days enjoying the present, and happily, idly pondering the future. I didn't worry so much about her anymore. Maybe I got a little less cynical. Maybe I smiled a little wider and a little bit more often, and maybe the sky looked a little bluer; the grass a little more green.

I had no way of knowing what or who decided how we lived, or how long we lived, or what the consequences of our actions and decisions were. I would almost certainly never know. When I died, I wouldn't know what chain of events had led directly to my death, and I wouldn't know what I would've been able to do to change it, or even if it ever could've been changed. Bad things were inevitable. Death was inevitable. But maybe the reverse was true: that good things were equally inevitable. And maybe sometimes inevitability liked to take a back seat to second chances.

Though I knew it couldn't last forever, I decided it was about time I let myself be happy. I was alive. Chloe was alive. Robbie was alive, and my father was alive and dating a woman who was well on her way to becoming his fiancée. And although it'd taken me a while to warm up to Deborah, I knew now that if Mom had been able to meet her, she'd have approved.

And for the time being, at least... all of that was good enough for me.

About the Author

Siera Maley has always loved writing, especially when it comes to what she thinks is missing in bookstores: quality young adult lesbian fiction. She first published *Time It Right* in 2013 and, thanks to many wonderful reviewers, followed it up with *Dating Sarah Cooper* in 2014, and *Taking Flight* and *On the Outside* in 2015. *Colorblind* is her fifth novel.

When she's not writing, Siera lives in the heart of Georgia with her girlfriend and their two adorable dogs.

You can visit her online at www.sieramaley.com or www.twitter.com/sieramaley.

CPSIA information can be obtained
at www.ICGtesting.com
Printed in the USA
LVOW11s1211260217
525462LV00009B/782/P